STRICTLY CONFIDENTIAL
Attraction

BRENDA JACKSON

Silhouette *Desire*

Published by Silhouette Books

America's Publisher of Contemporary Romance

Special thanks and acknowledgment are given
to Brenda Jackson for her contribution to
the TEXAS CATTLEMAN'S CLUB:
THE SECRET DIARY series.

 SILHOUETTE BOOKS

ISBN 0-373-76677-7

STRICTLY CONFIDENTIAL ATTRACTION

Visit Silhouette Books at www.eHarlequin.com

Printed in U.S.A.

Dear Reader

Silhouette Desire has a fantastic selection of novels for you this month, starting with our latest DYNASTIES: THE ASHTONS title, *Condition of Marriage* by Emilie Rose. Pregnant by one man…married to another, sounds like another Ashton scandal to me! *USA TODAY* bestselling author Peggy Moreland is back with a brand-new TANNERS OF TEXAS story. In *Tanner Ties,* it's a female Tanner who is looking for answers…and finds romance instead.

Our TEXAS CATTLEMAN'S CLUB: THE SECRET DIARY also continues this month with Brenda Jackson's fabulous *Strictly Confidential Attraction,* the story of a shy secretary who gets the chance to play house with her supersexy boss. Sheri WhiteFeather returns with another sexy Native American hero. You fell for Kyle in Sheri's previous Silhouette Bombshell novel, but just wait until you get to really know him in *Apache Nights.*

Two compelling miniseries also continue this month: Linda Conrad's *Reflected Pleasures,* the second book in THE GYPSY INHERITANCE—a family with a legacy full of surprises. And Bronwyn Jameson's PRINCES OF THE OUTBACK series has its second installment with *The Rich Stranger*—a man who must produce an heir in order to maintain his fortune.

Here's hoping this September's selections give you all the romance, all the drama and all the sensationalism you've come to expect from Silhouette Desire.

Melissa Jeglinski

Melissa Jeglinski
Senior Editor
Silhouette Desire

Please address questions and book requests to:
Silhouette Reader Service
U.S.: 3010 Walden Ave., P.O. Box 1325, Buffalo, NY 14269
Canadian: P.O. Box 609, Fort Erie, Ont. L2A 5X3

Books by Brenda Jackson

Silhouette Desire

Delaney's Desert Sheikh #1473
A Little Dare #1533
Thorn's Challenge #1552
Scandal between the Sheets #1573
Stone Cold Surrender #1601
Riding the Storm #1625
Jared's Counterfeit Fiancée #1654
Strictly Confidential Atttraction #1677

*Westmoreland family titles

BRENDA JACKSON

is a die "heart" romantic who married her childhood sweetheart and still proudly wears the "going steady" ring he gave her when she was fifteen. Because she's always believed in the power of love, Brenda's stories always have happy endings. In her real-life love story, Brenda and her husband of thirty-three years live in Jacksonville, Florida, and have two sons.

A *USA TODAY* bestselling author of over thirty romance titles, Brenda divides her time between family, writing and working in management at a major insurance company. You may write Brenda at P.O. Box 28267, Jacksonville, FL 32226, by e-mail at WriterBJackson@aol.com or visit her Web site at www.brendajackson.net.

ACKNOWLEDGMENTS

To my husband and best friend, Gerald Jackson, Sr.

To the members of the Brenda Jackson Book Club.
This one is for you.

And thanks to my Heavenly Father
who gave me the gift to write.

Prologue

From the diary of Jessamine Golden
September 12, 1910

Dear Diary,

Brad and I had another picnic on the lake today and there, beneath the branches of the willow tree, he told me that he loved me. His words stole my breath and everything around us got silent with such a profound statement from him. Then he gave me a heart-shaped pendant that was etched with two intertwining roses. Engraved on the back were our initials and he said his gift would always be a symbol of the love we share.

His words and gift brought tears to my eyes and when I told him how much I loved him, he pulled me into his arms and held me like he never wanted to let me go. And he kissed me in that special way of his that makes me want to be with him always and give up my quest for vengeance.

But I can't.

The circumstances as they are, I know what we are sharing can't last forever, although I want it to, more than anything. But I have to be honest with myself and with him. Brad is a man of duty, honor bound to do the right thing, and I have made a vow of revenge which goes against everything the man that I love stands for.

Oh, diary, my life is filled with so much turmoil. The woman in me longs for Brad's kisses, his touch and the way he makes me feel. That part of me wants to take what he offered me today— a love greater than any I have ever known that will last for all eternity.

However, I can't forget what I must do before my father can truly rest in peace.

I had vowed not to give my heart to any man before I settled a score, but it is too late. I feel the loving heat of the pendant as it rests between my breasts while I pen this entry. Brad Webster has my heart and I am deeply torn between love and duty.

One

"I need you, Alli."

Alison Lind's breath caught and she looked up from the papers in her hand and met the intense hazel eyes of Mark Hartman, convinced she had misheard his words.

Her heart flipped automatically whenever he did more than give her a casual glance. His teakwood-brown complexion held features that were rugged, sexy, mesmerizing. Broad-shouldered with a muscular build, he stood tall at a height of six foot one, and whenever he spoke in his deep, husky voice, her pulse raced.

She had secretly loved her handsome boss ever since he had returned to Royal, Texas, two years ago to open his self-defense studio and she had been hired as his secretary. Recently, he had changed her job title to administrative assistant, and the only time he'd ever indicated that he needed her was when he summoned her to his office to confirm an appointment or to discuss some other urgent business matter.

Inhaling in a deep breath, she held his gaze and asked in a hesitant voice, "You need me?"

"Yes," he said, coming around to sit on the edge of his desk. "Desperately."

How I wish, she thought staring at him, trying to keep the heat of desire from showing in her face; and trying even harder not to notice the way his jeans stretched tight across firm, muscular thighs. There was no doubt in her mind a miscommunication was taking place and he hadn't meant the words the way she hoped. In all honesty, there was no reason her insides should be feeling all giddy and she wished she could stop that warmth from intensifying between her legs. Too bad the attraction was one-sided. The majority of the time, Mark acted as if he didn't know she was alive. To him, she was his ever-efficient administrative assistant and nothing more.

Alli took another deep breath and asked, "You need me for what purpose?"

"Erika."

She raised an eyebrow. "You need me for Erika? I don't understand." Erika was Mark's eleven-month-old niece. He had become her legal guardian three months ago when his only brother and sister-in-law were killed in a car accident. Thoughts of the little girl sent a soft feeling through Alli. Erika was such a darling little girl and captured the hearts of all those who came in contact with her.

Alli watched as Mark blew out a breath before answering her. "I'm at the end of my rope and I don't know what to do or where to turn. As you know I've been having babysitting issues ever since Mrs. Tucker left to take care of her elderly parents in Florida. It may be months before she returns, if ever. So far I haven't been able to hire a dependable, not to mention competent, sitter. Yesterday was the last straw when I dropped by the ranch unexpectedly to find Erika's caregiver too absorbed in her soap opera to notice that Erika had crawled away and was outside on the patio, just a few feet from the pool. I told the woman a hundred times to always keep the door to the patio closed but she had forgotten. Yesterday wasn't the first time it's slipped her memory."

Alli shuddered. She didn't want to think about what might have happened had Erika tumbled into the pool, but looking at Mark, it was evident that he had thought about it. "You let the woman go." It was a statement and not a question. She couldn't imagine anyone being that careless where a child was concerned.

"Yes, immediately."

Alli nodded. "Who's keeping Erika today?"

"Christine. She's been kind enough to be Erika's backup sitter. Lately I've been using her more than I had intended. Now that she and Jake are engaged I'm sure she has more to do with her time than watch Erika for me."

Alli had to agree. Christine Travers was one of her closest friends in Royal and had become engaged to Jacob Thorne a couple of months ago. Christine had mentioned that she had taken care of Erika a few times and that she had enjoyed doing so. Alli knew all about Christine's busy schedule, especially since Jake was running for mayor and Christine was his campaign manager.

Alli met Mark's gaze. "You still haven't told me what specifically you need me for." For a moment he stayed silent as he studied her and Alli felt the increase of her pulse as the seconds ticked by.

"I know it's a lot to ask, but you're the only person I know I can truly depend on. I've watched you with Erika before when I've brought her into the studio. Not only that, I've seen you with other kids when the mothers come by for their classes and assume we have babysitting service. You're a natural, Alli. Kids take to you and you are the most responsible person I know."

Alli shrugged. His words weren't exactly the accolades she wanted to hear from the man she loved, but something was better than nothing. Besides, he was right. Her ability to care for children came naturally. She had grown up in a household with her mother and her baby sister Kara, who was seven years younger. Her father had abandoned his wife and daughters when Alison was twelve and never looked back. To make ends meet, Alli's mother had worked two jobs, leaving Alison to take care of Kara the majority of the time. When her mother had died right before Alli's seventeenth birthday, Alli had become Kara's sole caretaker. She couldn't help but smile knowing that Kara was doing wonderfully now in her second year of college at Texas Southern University in Houston.

"I'm asking you to be Erika's nanny."

Mark's words cut into Alison's thoughts and she blinked and looked at him, hoping she had heard wrong. "Excuse me?"

Mark met her gaze. Held it. "I need you to be Erika's nanny, which means you'll have to move in with me at the ranch and—"

"Whoa, wait a minute," Alli said, coming to her feet.

"There's no way I can do that. Have you forgotten that I work every day? I'm your assistant. I'm needed here and—"

Mark held up a hand, cutting her off. "Erika and I need you at the ranch with us even more, Alli. You're the only person I can depend on. The only person I can trust to take care of her. Knowing what could have happened yesterday took a good twenty years off my life. If anything had happened to her…"

Alli swallowed the lump in her throat. She was seeing a side of Mark she had never seen before, a vulnerable side. It was clearly evident that Erika had wiggled her way into her uncle's heart. When his brother and sister-in-law had been killed so unexpectedly, Mark hadn't been prepared to become a parent at twenty-eight, yet he was doing so and was trying to take care of Erika as best he could. But still there were obstacles in the way of what Mark was asking her to do and she decided to point them out to him.

"I'm majoring in computer engineering and attending college two nights a week—Tuesdays and Thursdays."

"I'll make sure I'm at home those nights so that won't be a problem."

Fat chance, Alison thought. He was asking her to move in with him at the ranch, which was a major problem. She was in love with him for Pete's sake. How could she handle being in such close proximity to him? Working with him at the self-defense studio was bad enough; but she wasn't sure she would survive sharing living quarters with him. Although she knew from the one time she had dropped off papers for him to sign that the Hartman Ranch was a huge place, the idea that they would be living under the same roof was unsettling.

"What about my work here?" she decided to ask.

"I'll go through an employment agency and find a temporary replacement. I'm willing to pay you double what you are making here."

Alison's eyes widened. "Double?"

"You heard me right. As Erika's nanny I'll pay you double. I need you just that much and as far as I'm concerned what you'll be doing is invaluable. You can't put a price on peace of mind."

Alison sat back down. *Double?* She breathed in deeply. As his administrative assistant she was getting paid what she thought was a very good salary, but she could certainly use the extra money for Kara's tuition. Kara had gotten a scholarship but that hadn't been enough to cover all the expenses. Alison had gone into her savings the last two semesters and if an emergency was to come up any time soon, she definitely would be in a tight spot. What Mark was offering would put more than a boost in her savings.

"And there will be a bonus."

Alison glanced up and met Mark's gaze. Once again his words had grabbed her attention. "A bonus?"

"Yes. One thousand dollars up-front just for agreeing to what I'm offering."

Stunned, Alison went speechless for a moment. *One thousand dollars?* That was money she could use to put down on another car. She was still driving the one she had bought right out of high school seven years ago, and lately it had been giving her problems. Just last week she had broken down while coming from class. Luckily, someone had stopped to help her, although the man had given her the creeps most of the time he'd been doing so.

She breathed in deeply. Mark was making his proposal hard to resist. And that in itself was the key word. *Resist.* For two years she had had to resist him, refusing to give into temptation and sharing her feelings. Instead she had fought her attraction and fully intended to continue to do so. She knew the last thing she needed was to place herself in a position where her heart could be broken if she assumed too much. But still, what he said was true. He and Erika needed her and there was no way she could not help him out. And she couldn't overlook the fact that he was helping her out financially as well.

"This will be a temporary arrangement, right?" Alison asked, feeling the need to have that point clarified.

"Yes. I'm hoping Mrs. Tucker is coming back to Royal in another month or so."

"And if she doesn't?"

"Then I'll run another ad in the paper and pray the results are better. There has to be someone in Royal who's responsible enough to keep Erika every day."

Alison nodded. "Will it really be necessary for me to move in with you and Erika at the ranch? I can stay at my place and drive to your—"

"No, I prefer for you to be there at the ranch with us. I may have business to take care of at night."

Alison nodded again. She was fully aware that he was a member of the Texas Cattleman's Club. Membership in the state's most exclusive club was restricted to wealthy ranchers, prestigious businessmen and oil tycoons. She'd heard that the members would often get together a few nights a week to play cards, share drinks and discuss business. But most of the good people of Royal knew that wasn't all they did. There were those who claimed through the generations, the club members had accepted the responsibility for the town's security and over the years had put their lives on the line for justice and peace. The only thing Alli did know for certain was that the club did great things for the community in the way of fund-raisers like the annual Cattleman's Ball, where the proceeds went to various charities.

Christine had talked Alison into attending Royal's Anniversary Ball that had occurred several weeks ago, and she had to admit that she had enjoyed herself…at least until Mark had arrived. Once he had walked into the room, she had found herself constantly watching him, as every other unattached woman had done. And as usual, he hadn't noticed her.

"So will you do it?"

Anytime and anyplace with you, she wanted to say. She hated her wanton thoughts, but when it came to Mark Hartman, they just wouldn't go away. She sighed deeply and did what she always did whenever her thoughts toppled onto the side of fantasy instead of reality, which was to scold herself inwardly and get back on track. Mark didn't have a single clue about how she felt about him and she intended to keep it that way.

"Alli? Will you help me out?"

She met his gaze and almost drowned in the plea she saw in his eyes. He did need her, or at least, thought he did. And although it wasn't in the way she wanted, it would have to do.

She stood and smiled. "Yes, Mark, I will help you out with Erika."

* * *

Half an hour later, Mark released a deep breath when Alli walked out of the room, closing the door behind herself. Both elated and frustrated, he moved away from his desk to walk over to the window. The plans had been finalized. He had contacted a reputable temp agency who would be sending someone in the morning. Alli was to train the person and by tomorrow evening she would be ready to move in with him and Erika, which was both a curse as well as a blessing.

From the first moment that Jake had told Mark about Alli and how efficient she would be as his secretary, he had been eager to interview her for the position. When he had seen her, he had gone almost speechless and had immediately known things wouldn't work out because of the sudden attraction he felt toward her. But he had needed a good secretary and everyone in town claimed she would be the best. Although she was a private person, most people knew her from working as a secretary for the Royal school system.

He had hired her on the spot, presenting her with a higher salary than she had been receiving. That was one move he hadn't regretted making. She had been the efficient, if shy, Alison Lind during the early months and had been instrumental in helping to get his studio off the ground. She had done the marketing, promotion, advertising, accounting…just about everything, freeing him to do what he did best, which was teaching the art of self-defense, primarily to women.

To him it was important that all women knew how to protect themselves. He doubted he would ever forgive himself for not being around when his wife had been attacked and killed while leaving the shopping mall late one night. As part of the marine's special forces, he had been away on a mission in the Middle East at the time. He knew he could not bring Patrice back, but maybe what he was doing would help other women who found themselves in a similar situation.

His thoughts shifted back to Alli. During the two years that they had worked together, he had tried like hell not to notice her, not to be attracted to her, not to want her. And for a while he thought he had gotten his pretended nonchalance down to an art form. But then all it would take was for him to walk out of his office and catch her unaware of being watched, as she filed away some document on a high shelf. He'd notice what a gorgeous pair of legs she had, or admire her small waist, pert and firm breasts and curvy thighs, and his nonchalance would be history.

And now she had agreed to move in with him.

His blood heated at the thought, but he quickly cooled it down. Whether Alli worked for him here at Hartman's Self-Defense Studio or at his home as Erika's nanny, their relationship would remain a business one. A serious relationship with any woman was the last thing he wanted or deserved. He had not been there to protect Patrice and, as a result, a part of him felt he couldn't be trusted to keep women safe. No woman needed a man who wasn't trustworthy, so living the rest of his life alone was something he accepted.

Well, he wasn't actually alone, he thought as a smile touched his lips. A few months ago he had been living the life of a carefree bachelor and hadn't been prepared for eight-month-old Erika Danielle Hartman. The first question that had come to his mind was what in the hell was he supposed to do with a kid? But soon the answers had come. He was to do just what his brother Matthew and his wife Candice had known Mark would do. He would provide not only a home for their daughter, but also he would make sure she received every good thing life had to offer, which was something he definitely could afford to do since, during his grandparents' time, oil had been discovered on their property, making the Hartmans instant millionaires.

He glanced at his watch when he heard the sound of the phone. He was expecting a call from Jake. His friend certainly had his plate full with the mayoral campaign while being an active member of the Texas Cattleman's Club, especially now when there were a number of strange things happening in Royal.

Mark reached his desk and quickly picked up the phone. Alli had already left for the day. "Yes?"

"Mark, this is Jake. There will be a meeting at the club tomorrow night at eight. Think you can make it?"

"Yes, I'll be there."

"What about Erika? Do you need Chrissie to watch her for you?"

"No, Alli has agreed to be Erika's nanny until Mrs. Tucker returns or until I can find someone dependable."

"Alli?"

"Yes."

"She's going to be both your assistant and Erika's nanny?"

Mark smiled, knowing Jake was confused. "No. I'm getting someone from a temp agency to handle the assistant duties for a while. Alli will be Erika's full-time nanny."

"Well, hell, Mark, how did you talk her into something like that?"

Mark sat in his desk chair as he thought about Jake's question. "I simply told her that Erika and I needed her." After a short pause he then said, "I also told her I would double what she was making here and I even threw in a bonus of a thousand dollars."

"Whew, you sound like a desperate man."

"When it comes to Erika's well-being, I am."

"Are you sure that you're only thinking about Erika. I can clearly recall your reaction to seeing Alli that night at the Anniversary Ball."

Mark leaned back in his chair. It was at times like this that he wished Jake had a short memory. He couldn't help but remember how speechless he had gotten when he had seen Alli the night Jake was referring to. She had looked nothing like his efficient, shy assistant. She had taken out the knot that she usually wore in her hair and the thick, silky strands had flowed around her shoulders. And that dress…wow! Seeing her in that dress would be forged in his mind as a delectable memory. On any other woman it would have been a simple black dress, but on Alison Lind there hadn't been anything simple about it. He had found himself drinking an entire glass of wine before realizing he had done so while staring at her.

"Okay, so I found her attractive that night. What of it?" he finally asked.

Jake chuckled and then said, "Nothing of it. I'll see you at the meeting tomorrow night. I understand that we have a lot to discuss. Logan heard from Nita Windcroft again today."

Mark rubbed a hand down his face. "She still thinks the Devlins are behind the mischief going on at her place?"

"Yes, and of course the Devlins are still claiming they know nothing about anything."

Mark shook his head. Having grown up in Royal, he knew that Windcrofts and Devlins had been feuding for years. He couldn't help but wonder if perhaps Nita was blowing things out of proportion, given her temper and her obvious dislike of the Devlins. "And what about Jonathan's death? Any new leads?"

It had been discovered a few months ago that instead of dying of a heart attack, Jonathan Devlin had been murdered with a lethal injection of potassium chloride. Sheriff Gavin O'Neal, who was also a member of the Texas Cattleman's Club, was leading the investigation into Jonathan's mysterious death.

"If there are any, Gavin will bring us up to speed. See you tomorrow."

After returning the telephone to its cradle, Mark stood and walked back to the window and stared out. Getting out of the marines after Patrice's death, he had decided to return to Royal to escape the memories. Within a short period of time he had become a member of the Texas Cattleman's Club, a front for members who worked together covertly on secret missions to save innocent lives.

Investigating Jonathan Devlin's death, as well as the incidents Nita Windcroft claimed were happening at her horse ranch, were keeping them busy. Then on top of everything else, there were still the mysteries surrounding the vandalism of the Edgar Halifax display and the map that had been stolen from the Royal Museum.

The latter bothered him more than anything because he had been assigned to keep an eye on the map while it was on the podium. However, he, like everyone else, had gotten distracted when a chandelier fell, nearly killing Melissa Mason, a television reporter, who'd been filming a scene that included the map. During that quick moment of chaos when fellow Cattleman Logan Voss had rushed across the room to save the woman he loved, thwarting an accident that could have been fatal, the map had vanished off the podium. Mark and his fellow club members were determined to get it back. The thief had been caught on film, but it turned out to be just a blurred image of a woman.

And speaking of images… The faces of two females filled his mind. The first was a beautiful little girl who was under his protection and the other was a stunningly attractive woman who could get under his skin if he wasn't careful.

Two

As Alli passed the huge wooden marker of the Hart-man Ranch, she couldn't help but ask herself for the umpteenth time whether or not she was doing the right thing. That question was temporarily forgotten when Mark's home loomed into view. It was massive as well as beautiful and she easily could place her modest house inside of it three or four times over.

She recalled the only other time she had been to this ranch and how in awe she had been. She remembered hearing around town how his grandparents had struck oil on the property and, as a result, the Hartmans lives had changed forever.

She also remembered her mother complaining about Mark's father when he would contact her whenever he needed ironing done, which was something Alli's mother had done on occasion to earn extra money. Mildred Lind had often said that Nathaniel Hartman was a cold, heartless and bitter man who hadn't shown anyone—not even his two sons—any love or affection.

When Mark had returned to Royal and contacted her about becoming his secretary, she had been hesitant about working for him, thinking that if he was anything like his father, she would not want him as an employer. Eventually she had decided not to prejudge him. She had worked for him only a couple of weeks before discovering that, although he was a private person, he treated her with kindness and was fair. But it was evident there were demons eating at him.

More than once, especially around the holidays, she had caught an expression of pain and grief in his face and a part of her had regretted all the sadness he had endured in his life. Most of the people in town had heard about the tragedy that had happened to his wife, prompting him to return to Royal. She'd also heard that Mark blamed himself for her death and establishing the studio to teach women self-defense was a way to relieve some of that guilt.

And speaking of guilt, she couldn't help but remember the phone call she'd gotten from her sister that morning. Kara had been all excited about a guy she had met the night before at the library. Alli had listened to her sister go on and on about what a hottie he was and that he had asked her to a party this weekend. Upon hearing that, red flags had gone up in Alli's head, especially after remembering Kara had mentioned earlier in the week how much studying she had to do for a big exam she had next week. Alli had ended up giving Kara some sisterly advice, which included a reminder of how important getting a good education was. Evidently that had been the last thing Kara had wanted to hear and, needless to say, had ended the call quickly. Alli was left wondering if perhaps she had reacted prematurely and laid the lecture on too thick. Kara had concentrated fully on her studies during her first year at Texas Southern and Alli just didn't want her to lose focus now. And Alli especially didn't want this "hottie" to interfere with Kara's studies.

Alli took a deep breath as she brought her car to a stop in front of the huge ranch house with the sprawling front porch, and couldn't help but smile when the door opened and Mark stepped out with Erika in his arms.

Mark had heard the sound of a car approaching and when he had glanced out of the window and saw it was Alli, he had breathed a deep sigh of relief. He had seen her briefly that morning, long enough to introduce her replacement before returning to the ranch to relieve Christine of Erika.

As soon as he stepped onto the porch and watched Alli get out of her car, he was besieged again with thoughts that having her here wasn't a good idea. But it was the only option he had. "Glad you made it," he said, coming to a stop near the steps. She smiled up at him and, although he didn't want it to, his insides felt warm all over.

It didn't help matters when he got a whiff of her perfume. He had long ago accepted that it was the most seductive scent he'd ever come in contact with. She was wearing her hair down around her shoulders, the way he liked. The sunlight slanting on her head made the strands appear more chestnut than dark brown in color.

"I'm glad I made it, too," she said coming to meet him and automatically taking Erika out of his arms to hold her against her shoulder. His niece remembered Alli from the times he had brought her to the studio and went willingly, but then she did the same thing to everyone. It often bothered him how friendly Erika was and knew when she got older he would have to make sure he taught her not to be so open to strangers.

"You need help with your things?" Mark asked, seeing the boxes in the back seat of her car.

He studied the older vehicle and hoped she would use the bonus she would be getting to purchase another one. Recently he had overheard Christine telling Jake how the car had broken down on an isolated road leading into town one night and that Malcolm Durmorr had stopped to offer help.

Malcolm, known around town as a shiftless lowlife who was always on the brink of some kind of disaster, was said to be a distant cousin of the Devlins, although it seemed they weren't eager to claim him. There were a number of things about him that Mark didn't like, especially the get-rich-quick schemes Malcolm had pulled on a couple of innocent, unsuspecting people in Royal.

Mark recalled how Malcolm had come into the Royal Diner one afternoon and had sat eating his dinner while gazing at one particular waitress by the name of Valerie Raines as though he would have preferred having her on his plate instead of the pork chop. The lust in the man's eyes had been disgusting and the thought that Malcolm had been the one to help Alli hadn't set too well with Mark.

Mark suddenly lost his train of thought when Erika,

fascinated with the gold chain around Alli's neck, reached inside Alli's blouse to pull out the topaz pendant attached to it, providing Mark with a generous view of Alli's cleavage as well as the top of a black lace bra. Upon realizing what the baby had done, Alli quickly switched Erica to her other shoulder and snatched the blouse back up in place. When Alli met his gaze, an embarrassing tint flushed her cheeks.

Mark thought it best to pretend he hadn't seen a thing instead of standing there wishing he could get an instant replay. He cleared his throat. "If you give me your keys, I'll bring your stuff inside so you can get settled in," he said as warning bells clanged in his ears.

He had to fight his attraction to Alli no matter what, but already things were getting off to a heated start. With her dressed in a blouse and a pair of slacks wasn't helping. He had decided after the first time he had seen Alli in pants that she'd had the most well-defined, enticingly shaped butt of any woman he'd ever seen. In fact, he didn't know of anyone who even qualified as a close second.

She always dressed professionally while in the office. The only time he hadn't seen her dressed that way was when she had signed up to take his class. He remembered how, like the other ladies, she had shown up wearing shorts. In addition to teaching her the art of self-defense, he had taught himself the art of self-control.

His thoughts returned to the present when she handed him her car key. "I didn't bring over much since I'll have time to do more packing this weekend," she said shifting her gaze from him to Erika. "Has she eaten dinner yet?"

Mark laughed. "Yes. If she was hungry, you would know it. That's the only time she's in a bad mood."

Alli gave herself a mental shake. Mark's laugh threw her, since she had never heard him laugh before. This was the first time she had ever seen this side of him. He was being so pleasant and human. Not that he walked around being a tyrant, but he'd never been in her presence and not acted with reserve and reticence.

He must have seen the strange look on her face because he eyed her for a moment as his expression went from curious to concern. Then he asked, "Is something wrong?"

She shrugged. "No, nothing's wrong." Cautiously, she added, "I just don't ever recall the two of us ever holding a conversation for more than five minutes that didn't have anything to do with business."

Mark leaned against the wooden column and thought for a moment. Neither had he. Even yesterday while they had discussed the arrangements of her becoming Erika's nanny, it had been business. "Well, you're doing me a huge favor by being here. Away from work I'm more relaxed and at ease so get prepared to see another side of me. Believe it or not, I can be a friendly guy."

"It's not that I thought you weren't friendly," Alli rushed to say, hoping she hadn't offended him. "But you—"

He held up his hand. "Hey, there's no need to explain," Mark said chuckling, thinking he liked how Alli looked when she was flustered, which was something he rarely had seen. "Come on in, let me show you around. I'll get the things out of your car later."

She gave him her usual shy smile and said, "All right."

Erika began murmuring words Alli couldn't quite make out as she followed Mark into the house. This was her first time inside. The last time she had been here he had stepped out onto the porch to sign the papers she had delivered.

She glanced around as Mark took her from room to room. She couldn't help noticing how each one was richly furnished with leathered pieces of a rustic, western design. Erika's bedroom was another matter. It was wallpapered with Snow White and her seven dwarfs, and a beautiful white convertible crib sat in the middle of the room. The room's decor was colorful, bright, fit for a little princess, and the bedding accessories matched a miniature chair and ottoman that sat near a window in the room. A huge stuffed bear had been placed in the chair. Alli couldn't help smiling. "It's beautiful in here, Mark."

He turned to her. "Thanks. I hired a professional decorator for this room. I was a bachelor with no experience with kids when I got Erika and had to learn everything and fast."

He automatically took Erika out of Alli's arms when his niece reached for him. He nodded toward all the furniture in the room "The first thing I found out was that a child's room should grow with the child and not the child having to grow with the room. I spend a lot of time in here with Erika since this is also her play room," he said, tipping his head toward the huge toy chest that sat in one corner. "That's the reason for the recliner-rocker over there. When I first got her I would sit in that chair and rock her to sleep. Now I just sit back and watch her play."

Alli nodded as she studied the chair, seeing the image of Mark kicked back, relaxed, while keeping a protective eye on Ericka. Another vision suddenly came to mind: one of her sitting in that chair with him, in his lap, while the two of them watched Erika together. She could actually see herself as she cuddled close to him, her body curled to his with her head resting on his shoulder, while the warmth of his breath fanned her face.

She blinked and swallowed deeply, not believing she had allowed such thoughts to enter her mind.

"Alli, are you okay?"

She snapped her head around and met Mark's curious eyes. "Yes, I'm fine."

It seemed that he focused his gaze on her for the longest time before saying, "Okay, then let me show you the room that you'll be using."

Before they walked out the room they passed a framed picture sitting on the dresser. Alli stopped and picked it up. It was a photograph of an attractive couple who were smiling and holding an infant.

"That's Matt and Candice when Erika was only a few months old," Mark said softly.

Alli stiffened slightly. She hadn't been aware that he was standing so close. He was leaning down to peer at the picture and she could feel the moist warmth of his breath against her neck. His closeness was causing a sensation she had never felt before to slowly inch its way up her spine. There was also the heat she felt pooling her belly.

She forced herself to stay focused on the picture, fearful that if she turned her head even the slightest inch, her lips would connect to his. "They were a beautiful family and look happy together," she finally said, forcing the words out while keenly aware the heat had moved from her stomach, traveling lower down her body.

"Yes, they were happy together and they loved each other very much. I always envied what they had."

Noting that Mark had taken a step back, Alli turned slightly and met his gaze. He'd sounded so heartrending. She couldn't help looking deep into his eyes, and then she saw it clearly—pain. He was still hurting. But for whom? His brother and sister-in-law? His wife? For all three?

Her gaze shifted to the rest of his features. They were prominent. Handsome. He had beautiful brown skin, thick eyebrows, a nose that was the perfect shape and size for his face. And then there were his lips…

She couldn't help but study his lips. They had a seductive shape to them and had such a smooth texture. They looked soft, which seemed odd for such a rough man. A part of her yearned to figure out the contrast for herself. It wouldn't take much for her to ease her mouth to his, take her tongue and go from corner to corner and lick the—

"Da-da! Down da-da!"

Erika's words snapped Alli around. She had no idea just how long she had been standing there mesmerized by Mark's mouth. What had he thought of her staring at him like that? Heat flooded her cheeks and, instead of meeting his gaze, she placed the picture frame on the dresser.

"No, I can't put you down, sweetheart," she heard Mark say to the baby. "We still have to show Alli around."

Feeling more in control, Alli turned but kept her gaze focused on Erika and smiled when the little girl reached for her. She scooped her out of Mark's arms and planted a kiss on Erika's cheek, liking the sound of her giggle. "She calls you dad."

"Yes, but I prefer that she didn't do that."

The agitation in his voice made Alli's head jerk up, not being able to avoid eye contact with him any longer. She saw the deep frown that marred his handsome features. "Why?" she asked.

"Because I'm not her daddy."

Alli lifted an eyebrow in confusion. "I know you're not her daddy, Mark, but calling you that is as natural and familiar to her as eating and sleeping. You represent a permanent fixture in her life. She might or might not remember her parents and—"

"I want her to remember them, Alli. That's the reason I have this picture in here. When she gets older I want her to know about them. I want her to know they were her parents and that I'm her uncle who's nothing more than her caretaker."

Alli tried not to glare at him but felt herself doing so anyway. What he'd said sounded too detached and she knew that wasn't the case. Anyone could see how much he loved and adored his niece. Alison had been in his office when he had received the call regarding his brother's and sister-in-law's deaths and his being named as Erika's guardian. That had to have been a tailspin for any carefree bachelor.

She would never forget the day he had flown to California to bring his niece home. And it was obvious he was fiercely protective of Erika, otherwise Alli wouldn't be here.

Pursing her lips, Alli studied Erika's features then met Mark's gaze. "She favors you a lot. You both have identical hazel eyes, the same skin coloring, and her mouth is like yours, just a smaller version. She could be your daughter."

He stuck his hands in the pockets of his jeans and rocked on his heels. She had worked with him long enough to know the first signs of his anger. "But she's not. You saw the photograph. Matt and I looked alike but there was a lot about us that was different. We were both Nathaniel Hartman's sons so there were some things that couldn't be changed, but Matt inherited a lot of Mama's ways. Although the old man tried making him hard, Matt had a soft spot. And he always wanted to grow up and have children. I never did."

Mark's words surprised Alli. He was sharing more with her now than he had before. "But how could you not want kids? You were married."

Mark stared at her in silence for a moment, reached out and absently took Erika out of her arms. He moved to put space between them. Moments later he said, "Getting married had nothing to do with it. Patrice knew I never wanted kids, which was fine with her since, because of a medical condition, she couldn't have them."

Alli felt her pulse go still and she inhaled a deep breath. It appeared that this was a touchy subject with Mark but she wasn't ready to put it to rest. She crossed the room to join him and Erika. "Now that Erika has broken you in, what do you think about fatherhood?"

His head shot around and hazel eyes collided with hers. Too late she realized what she'd asked was a mistake. "I'm Erika's uncle, let's keep that clear, Alli. Matt entrusted her into my care and I will do the best that I can by her. She will never want for anything. And as far as me ever wanting kids of my own, nothing has changed. I still don't want any."

Alli's chest tightened as he placed Erika in her arms and she watched him walk out of the room.

Three

It was the most stunning room, Alli thought, as she followed Mark into the bedroom that was conveniently located across the hall from Erika's.

Besides the huge four-poster, cherry-oak bed that sat between two huge windows, the other furnishings included double nightstands, a mirror dresser, a chest and an accent bench. All in all the elegant-looking accessories, from the floral bedspread and matching window treatments to the massive brick fireplace, and she felt it was a room fit for a queen. What was even nicer was the fact that she had her own bath, a rather nice modern one that had a separate shower and a bathtub. It was apparent some renovations been done since the original house had been built.

"I hope you like this room."

She swung around and the swift movement made

Erika happily squeal loudly. "Oh, Mark, it's perfect. Did you hire a professional decorator to do this room as well?"

He nodded. "Yes, when I moved back I found the place needed a lot of repairs." He took Erika out of Alli's arms and continued saying, "After the repairs were taken care of I started doing renovations. I wanted to give the place a whole new look and I didn't want anything here to remind me of before."

A part of Alli wanted to reach out and throw her arms around him. She regretted he did not have memories of a happy childhood. Although her father had deserted them and her mother had eventually worked herself into an early grave, Mildred Lind had done the best she could to make sure her daughters had childhoods filled with many fond memories. There hadn't been a lot of money to spend but there had been a lot of love to go around. Too bad Mark had missed out on that.

"I'd better get your things out the car," Mark said, handing Erika back to her.

Alli chuckled as she held Erika against her shoulder. Mark lifted an eyebrow in confusion. "What's so funny?"

"Have you noticed what we've been doing? I bet Erika has never been passed back and forth before between two people so much in her life."

A smile touched the corners of Mark's lips. "You're probably right. I hadn't noticed."

Alli smiled at Erika before dropping a kiss on her cheek. "But you noticed didn't you, sweetheart, and you enjoyed every minute of going from arm to arm, right?"

"That's something else she isn't used to."

Alli switched her gaze to Mark. "What?"

"Being kissed. You've done it three times since you've been here."

Forcing her gaze back to Erika, Alli asked, "You're counting?"

He shrugged. "I can't help but notice. I didn't know you were such an affectionate person."

There's a lot you don't know about me, Mark Hartman. She looked at him, wanting to tell him that she had more than enough affection to share if he was interested, but she knew that saying that wouldn't be a good idea. "Well, when it comes to babies, I'm as affectionate as anyone can get."

"You want children one day?"

She grinned. "You would have done better just asking me how many."

After studying her thoughtfully for a brief moment, he said, "Okay, how many?"

"A houseful. I'll even make room in the barn if I have to."

Evidently the image of that played out in Mark's mind and he chuckled. "I hope your husband will be able to afford all your kids."

"I hope so, too." Automatically and without thought, she kissed Erika's cheek again, making the baby giggle with pleasure.

When Alli glanced up she saw that Mark's gaze was focused on her lips while he absently wet his own with his tongue. She became aware of the tension that suddenly filled the room and the pulsing heat that was forming between them. As if his lips were dry, he licked them again and at that moment she was dying to know how his kisses tasted.

Alli was mortified that such thoughts had entered her mind and knew she should dismiss them, but she couldn't. Even if she were to kiss him until the cows came home, he would never be out of her system...or out of her heart. He was still staring at her mouth the way she was staring at his. The beatings of their hearts could be heard as a throbbing tempo in the room and even Erika's babbling couldn't drown it out.

Heat flowed all through her when she could see the guarded expression that he always wore was gone and he was staring at her as if he finally was seeing her as a woman. At that very moment, whether it was his intent or not, he made her feel desired. She wanted more than anything to curl up in his arms while he kissed her in all the ways she had dreamed about.

Her breath caught in her throat when he took a step closer, leaned forward and came within inches of capturing her mouth in his.

"Da-da. Play."

As if snapping out of a daze, Mark straightened, took a quick step back and ran a hand down his face. "I better get your things out the car," he said, turning quickly.

Emotions tightened Alli's throat. He had almost kissed her. After two years, he had shown some sign that he was attracted to her.

"You do remember about my Cattleman's Club meeting tonight, right?"

His question jarred her from her thoughts. "Yes, I remember."

"And don't worry about dinner. Mrs. Sanders was here yesterday and prepared enough dinner for today as well."

"Mrs. Sanders?"

"She's my housekeeper and cook, and she usually comes a couple of times a week."

Evidently seeing the question in her eyes, he went on to say, "She cooks and cleans but is quick to inform you that she doesn't do babies. She's fifty-seven, has five kids of her own and doesn't relish the thought of taking care of another child. She's one of those grandmothers whose kids can't just drop the grandkids off and keep going. Her philosophy is, and I quote, 'I raised mine, now you raise yours.'"

"I'm looking forward to meeting her," Alli said as she continued to stare at Mark. She thought it was a darn shame for any man to look that good. He took her breath away. She needed him to leave so she could breathe normally again.

He smiled warmly. "And I have a feeling that she's looking forward to meeting you as well."

And then he was gone.

"I hear you've solved your babysitting problems, Mark," Logan Voss said as the two of them entered the bar of the Texas Cattleman's Club and proceeded to the private meeting room.

Out of habit, Mark's gaze went to the Leadership, Justice and Peace motto on a far wall before meeting his friend's eyes. "Then I'm also sure you've heard that Alli is Erika's nanny."

Logan chuckled. "Yes, I did hear that."

"What did you hear?" Jake Thorne asked curiously

as he greeted the two men and watched them settle into the leather chairs.

"That Alli is Erika's nanny," Logan responded.

Jake smiled. "Yes, and knowing what a responsible person Alli is, we can safely say that Erika will be in good hands."

Mark nodded. At the moment, he would have given anything to know just how good those hands were; just as he would have loved sampling that mouth of Alli's. Luckily for him, when he had returned to the room with her things, she hadn't been there. She had placed Erika in her stroller and had taken her outside for a walk. He was grateful for that time alone to pull himself together. Never in his life had he wanted to kiss a woman so badly.

He had spent a long time in the shower berating himself for his weakness of coming within inches of kissing Alli. By the time he had gotten dressed for the meeting, he had decided that hell, he was only human, and any man would have wanted to kiss her given the way her lips were made, not to mention how alluring her perfume was. The total package would have any man interested and he was definitely a man.

Damn, he had to stop thinking about her. Thoughts of her had consumed him on the drive to this meeting and they were consuming him now. He hoped like hell that she'd be asleep when he returned home. But just in case, it might be a good idea if he didn't return to the ranch immediately after the meeting. Maybe he could interest a couple of the guys in a game of poker.

He glanced around. He knew Thomas Devlin and Gavin O'Neal were standing outside talking. But where the hell was Connor Thorne? He was the one who had ribbed Mark the most whenever he had shown up late due to babysitting issues. Mark wondered if Connor also had heard that his problem was solved.

Mark glanced over at Jake. "Where's Connor?"

Jake smiled lazily, his blue eyes shining brightly. "I am my brother's brother, but I am not my brother's keeper," he replied jokingly. He then glanced at his watch. "We have seven minutes to go. He'll be here."

Mark nodded and then asked, "How's the campaign going?" Jake's opponent in the mayoral race was Gretchen Halifax. In her mid-thirties, Gretchen was intelligent, sophisticated and had a large circle of influence in town. But what she didn't have was a clue about what Royal needed. If Gretchen became mayor, there was no doubt in Mark's mind that, with her proposed tax plan, the town would lose businesses to other areas.

"I'm playing by the rules and sticking to the campaign issues," Jake said. "But it seems Gretchen doesn't want to play fair."

Logan, who had stood to remove his jacket, sat and chuckled as he leaned back in his chair. "Now why doesn't that surprise me?"

The three men glanced up when Connor Thorne, Tom Devlin and Gavin O'Neal walked in. They could tell by the look on Gavin's face that the news he had to share wouldn't be good. As a relatively new sheriff, he had his hands full trying to figure out a murder as well as a number of suspicious happenings around town.

"We might as well get started," Gavin said, dropping into one of the leather chairs. Connor and Tom, who had recently joined the club, did likewise.

When Gavin was certain he had everyone's attention,

he continued to speak. "We still don't have a clue who fired that shot at Melissa Mason," he said to everyone, although the guys knew he was really answering the question Logan hadn't asked yet. Melissa was Logan's fiancée and the attempt on her life had riled him to say the least.

"So we're still operating on the theory that since Melissa was driving one of Logan's vehicles, the sniper thought it was Logan and was trying to dissuade him from going to see Lucas Devlin?" Connor asked, leaning forward.

"Yes. In my opinion someone is trying like hell to keep the Devlin and Windcroft feud going," Gavin said somberly.

"Hmm, but who would benefit from such a thing and how does it all tie in to Jonathan's murder?" Jake asked, as if thinking out loud.

"That's what we need to find out," Gavin said, sighing deeply. He glanced over at Mark. "I need you to go talk to Nita Windcroft to see whether her allegations are founded or she's blowing things out of proportion to stir up trouble. I'm fairly new to the area but what I'm hearing is that she's pretty damn headstrong and if she thinks we're not taking her seriously, she might take matters into her own hands. Heaven help us all if she does that. My deputies claim she has one hell of a temper and is as stubborn as they come."

Mark nodded. "All right. I'll talk to Nita."

Gavin then glanced over at Jake and smiled. "I thought I'd better give you a heads-up. Rumor has it around town that Gretchen is trying like hell to tie you to the vandalism of the Halifax Exhibit. She claims you're running a negative campaign and that's one example of your unsavory tactics."

Jake shook his head and chuckled. "Thanks for letting me know but if anyone is using unsavory tactics, it's Gretchen. But she'll eventually hang herself since the people who know me won't believe a word of it."

"What about the woman captured on tape stealing the map? Any new leads?" Tom Devlin decided to ask, his silver-gray eyes alert. Since he was relatively new to town, he was quickly finding out about the feud that involved the family he only recently had discovered he had.

"No, there's nothing new," Gavin said. "I showed the video around and no one seems to recognize the woman, so it's still a mystery." He glanced down at his watch. "That's all I have to report tonight. I'm sure you're all aware that word has gotten around that Jonathan was murdered by some sort of lethal injection and everyone has an idea of who did it." He shook his head. "You wouldn't believe how many people stopped me today with the list of their own suspects."

Mark lifted an eyebrow in amusement. "Any particular name that's heading the list?"

Gavin sighed. "Yeah, Nita Windcroft's, but only because of the feud. But then everyone was quick to add that more than likely she didn't do it because she would not have let poor Jonathan linger. If he had made her mad enough, she would have taken a gun and shot him on the spot."

Connor grinned. "She doesn't sound like a woman I would want to tangle with."

Tom chuckled. "From what I'm hearing, no one would."

Gavin smiled. "Well, that ends tonight's meeting. We'll get together again next Wednesday. At that time, Mark, you can tell us what you've found out after talking with Nita."

"Sure thing," Mark said." When the men all stood, he asked, "Anyone interested in a game of poker tonight?"

Jake smiled and shook his head. "Sorry, I have a lady waiting for my return."

"And so do I," Logan said, grinning as he put back on his jacket. His gray-green eyes had the quiet, determined intent of a man who knew just where he was going and didn't plan on wasting time getting there.

Mark studied the two men who were rushing for the door. "Hmm, I can distinctively remember a time when there were no ladies in your lives."

Jake paused in the doorway and chuckled. "Well, you know how it is." After studying Mark for a brief moment he said, "Then again, my friend, maybe you don't. But I have a feeling that one day soon you will." Then he was gone with Logan right on his heels.

Mark frowned and turned to look at Tom, Connor and Gavin. "What the hell did he mean by that?"

Gavin shrugged. "I'm through figuring out things for the night. I'll leave that one for the three of you to ponder." His brown eyes seemed to smile when he added, "I'm headed over to the diner for a cup of coffee." And he rushed out the door as well.

Mark, Connor and Tom shared a knowing look between them. They knew of Gavin's fascination with a certain waitress at the Royal Diner.

"The least he could have done was invite us to come along," Connor said jokingly.

"Yes, he very well could have. However, since he didn't, we can only assume he felt that four was a crowd," Tom replied laughing.

Mark nodded, amused. "Maybe I better warn Gavin that he's not the only one who has the hots for Valerie Raines. I've notice Malcolm Durmorr giving her a lusty eye more than once when I happened to be in there."

Connor sat and folded his arms over his chest, rolling his blue eyes heavenward. "Malcolm? That low-life?" He glanced over at Tom. "Sorry. I forgot he's a distant relative of yours."

Tom shook his head. "From what I understand, the Devlins try to forget that fact as well."

Connor seemed to understand. He then gave Mark a sly grin. "If I were you, I wouldn't tell Gavin anything about Malcolm's interest in Valerie Raines. Competition is good for the soul and it will keep our sheriff on his toes."

Mark smiled. "Maybe you're right." He glanced at his watch. It wasn't nine o'clock and chances were Alli hadn't gone to bed yet. He looked at Connor and Tom. "A game of poker anyone?"

When the two men agreed, Mark's smile widened. Good. He'd been saved by a poker game.

Holding Erika in her arms, Alli walked over to the rocker-recliner and sat. She could not believe that it was almost nine o'clock and the little girl was still wide awake. She couldn't help but smile down at the big, beautiful hazel eyes in that round little face that was staring up at her. Her dark curly hair framed her face and a little pink ribbon sat on top of her head.

Alli smiled as she shook her head thinking that every

time she'd seen Erika her hair had been fixed the same way, which was probably a convenient style for Mark. She decided that she was going to introduce Erika to some cute new hairdos and thought a mass of braids would look rather nice on her.

"So, your uncle is short on affection and you still love him anyway, huh?" Alli said as she began rocking the chair. "Well, I know just how you feel, so welcome to the club."

When the baby gave her a grin that showed a few sprouting teeth, Alli returned the gesture. "I guess it's going to take the two of us to give him a lesson in love, wouldn't you say?"

As Alli continued to rock, she thought that, affection or no affection, Mark was evidently doing something right for his niece to adore him so much. She had noted earlier while feeding Erika a snack that even the slightest sound had Erika glancing toward the kitchen door as if anxious to see her uncle walk through it. And a couple of times she had wandered around the living room chanting "Da-da" as if saying it would make Mark appear.

Okay, so he didn't go for all that kissy stuff, but he was bestowing affection on Erika in ways that Mark himself probably didn't even realize.

Like this rocker-recliner chair for instance.

He had mentioned how he used to rock her in it. An affectionless person would not have bothered doing that.

Alli sighed deeply. After what had almost happened between her and Mark in the bedroom, she had needed distance and a chance to escape. Spotting the stroller in Erika's room, she had decided it would be a perfect time to go for a stroll around the Hartman property.

She had never imagined the ranch consisted of that much land. It seemed she had walked endlessly, enjoying the beauty of the landscape and wondering how Mark had ever moved away since every tree, shrub and patch of grass was so beautiful. And Erika seemed to have enjoyed being outside, breathing in the rich Texas air and appreciating the warmth of a sunny September day.

Alli glanced down at the little girl who was still fighting sleep, although it seemed she wasn't winning as much as she had been earlier. "You have your uncle's heart and he doesn't even know it. He's so slow. A typical man," she whispered as she continued to rock.

Moments later she glanced down and saw that Erika had fallen asleep, but Alli wasn't ready to put her down yet. So she kept rocking and slowly her own eyes closed as thoughts of a very slow, typical man by the name of Mark Hartman filled her unconsciousness.

It was close to eleven o'clock when Mark returned to the ranch. As habit, he went straight to Erika's room to check on her and was surprised to find the light still on in her bedroom. He was further surprised to see Alli holding Erika in the rocker-recliner and they were both asleep.

He had seen Erika sleeping many times but this was the first time he had ever seen his administrative assistant anything but wide awake and fully alert. For a moment he couldn't move, too mesmerized by the beauty of her sitting there with her eyes closed. So he took the time to study her.

His gaze first went to her hair—thick, shoulder-length and dark brown. A vision entered his mind of him running his fingers though the silky strands while he was kissing her. His gaze then shifted to her face and took in the creaminess of her brown skin, the perfection of her naturally shaped eyebrows and the faultless precision of her chin. But what his gaze zeroed in on was her mouth. Even from across the room it looked moist, tempting, inviting.

He swallowed. His own lips suddenly felt hot, dry, parched and he was convinced that the only way to bring relief to them was to mate them with hers. Without questioning the wisdom of what he was about to do, he slowly crossed the room to her.

He leaned over and softly whispered in Alli's ear. "I'm putting Erika in her bed, Alli."

He watched as Alli's eyes flew open the moment he scooped his niece out of her arms. "Mark, you're back," she whispered and the low, throaty sound, as well as the sigh that followed, sent a riveting sensation all the way to his gut. And the sensuously seductive scent of her wasn't helping matters.

Holding Erika, he straightened and met Alli's eyes. "Yes, I'm back. Let me put her in bed."

He turned quickly and crossed the room to lay his niece down. Covering her with the blanket, he watched her for a moment to make sure she was all right and checked the monitor that was attached to the crib before turning his attention back to Alli.

She was standing and his throat tightened when he saw she was no longer wearing slacks but had changed into shorts. His desire was instantaneous and his gaze moved over her. Their eyes connected and he studied the darkness of her brown eyes and felt the same intense heat that he was feeling radiating from them. The same heat that was burning his insides with desire.

"I had meant to put her down earlier but fell asleep rocking her," she whispered.

"Did you?" he asked softly.

"Yes."

He slowly began walking over toward her.

Alli's pulse raced. He was looking at her that way again. The way he had earlier, which was the way he always looked at her in her dreams, especially the one he had awakened her from moments earlier. She knew she should be happy, thrilled and elated that after two years he was finally noticing her, but a part of her questioned the wisdom of becoming involved with Mark, although she was hopelessly in love with him.

When he came to a stop in front of her, his eyes leveled on hers. He reached out and lifted her chin with his finger. "You are a very beautiful woman, Alli."

She blinked, startled. She hadn't expected him to say such a thing. At first she didn't know what to say, then she decided to say something flippant, although being flip wasn't the norm for her. But it seemed that tonight neither she nor Mark was acting normally.

She smiled and tilted her head to the side. "So, it took you two years to notice, Mark?" she asked jokingly.

His eyes seemed to darken when he said, "No. I noticed the first day I met you, which is the reason I came pretty damn close to not hiring you."

His words wiped that glib look off her face. She then nibbled nervously on her lower lip. "I didn't think you noticed me."

He tilted her chin up more. "Oh, trust me, you've

been a distraction, Alli. In fact, for two years I've been fighting my attraction to you. And that night at the Anniversary Ball was the hardest, I think. You looked so damn beautiful in that gown and more than once I started to ask you to dance but stopped myself. The last thing I wanted when I returned to Royal was to become seriously involved with anyone, especially an employee."

Alli nodded. She hadn't known he had paid her any attention at the ball and knowing that he had filled her with happiness. "And now?" she asked quietly.

"And now I want to kiss you so bad I ache."

"Oh."

That was the only word he gave her time to say before he embraced her as his mouth descended on hers, stealing her next breath. At the same time, he swept his tongue into her mouth. And she accepted it with the same ease that he gave it to her.

Alli had never been kissed this way. If the truth were known, at twenty-five she had never really been kissed at all and was puzzled by how effortless it was to follow Mark's lead. Taking care of Kara had been a full-time job and left no time for dating. But she'd figured she had not missed out on anything...until now. She seriously doubted that anyone would have been able to blow her away with a kiss the way Mark was doing. He had the ability to turn on all her buttons and was sending new sensations zinging all through her. She wondered if he knew how much of a novice she was at this.

He did.

Mark had detected it the moment his tongue had entered Alli's mouth and he had felt her body go tense at the invasion, as if she hadn't been expecting such intimacy. He had kissed a lot of women, some more experienced than others. He wouldn't go so far to say that Alli had never been kissed before, but evidently the other men hadn't done it right.

Not only did he intend to do it right, but he also planned on taking it to another level. He pulled back slightly and whispered against her moist lips. "Wrap your arms around my neck, Alli."

She did as he asked and, the moment she complied with his request, he captured her mouth again and deepened the kiss while one of his hands stroked through her hair and the other wrapped around her waist, bringing her closer to the fit of him. He heard her moan softly and felt the way her heart was racing with her chest pressed so tightly to his. He also felt the firm tips of her breasts, which made his pulse quicken.

He knew the moment she became aware of his erection and, when she deliberately rocked into him, he released a low groan and automatically thrust his hips against hers. He had asked her to place her arms around his neck but now she was clutching his shoulders, kneading her fingers deep into the muscles as if to keep her balance. The way she was returning his kiss was robbing him of any control he might have had. He lowered his arms from her waist to mold her curvy buttocks more intimately against him.

The sound of Erika whimpering in her sleep made Mark withdraw his mouth and inhale deeply. It also brought about a semblance of self-control. He took a step back and stared at Alli's swollen mouth, thinking this woman was all fire and danger. At the moment he didn't want to tangle with either. Kissing her had definitely been a mistake. Not only she was an affectionate person, but she was a passionate one as well. And it had been obvious from their kiss that her sensuality hadn't been tapped yet.

He dragged in another deep breath and with it came a whiff of her perfume. Seductive. Alluring. A total turn-on. Needing to put distance between them, he crossed the room to Erika's crib to check on her.

"Mark, we—"

"Made a mistake," he said briskly, finishing what he knew she was about to say. "Go on to bed, Alli. I'll see you in the morning," he all but snapped.

Out of the corner of his eyes, he saw how Alli's spine stiffened. He was tempted to go to her and start the kissing all over again. But he knew he couldn't do that.

Mark didn't turn around until he heard the sound of the door closing. It was then that he sat in the rocker-recliner and dropped his head into his hands, thinking that he finally had given into temptation. And as a result, he definitely had made a mess of things.

Four

He owed Alli an apology.

Mark awakened with that thought and quickly glanced at the clock on the nightstand beside his bed. It was still early, barely five in the morning. Chances were she was still sleep so, for the time being, there was nothing he could do.

He rubbed his hand down his face when the memory of kissing her seeped into his mind. Damn, she hadn't been in his house for a full night and he had acted like a stallion in heat. That had been unfair to her.

She was here to take care of his niece, something he appreciated her doing. But he had shown his gratitude by pouncing on her the first chance he'd gotten and would have continued kissing her if they hadn't been interrupted by the sounds Erika had made in her sleep.

Although he didn't want to, he found himself again

thinking about the kiss they had shared. He had wanted to taste Alli, and had gotten more than he'd bargained for. Her lips had fit perfectly to his, as if they had been made just for him, and they had felt soft and had had such a seductive flavor. And when he had deepened the kiss, he had wanted more than anything to pick her up, take her into his bedroom, place her on his bed, undress her and then slide inside of her, between her long shapely legs...

Mark muttered a curse as he threw back the covers to sit on the side of the bed. Since it seemed that going back to sleep was out of the question, he decided to get up. Although it was early, there were a number of things he could do before leaving for the studio. And no matter how many appointments he had on his calendar, he intended to give Nita Windcroft a call to determine the best time he could drive over to the Windcroft horse farm to talk to her.

But first thing this morning, as soon as he saw Alli, he intended to apologize for his actions last night.

Sitting on the accent bench in her bedroom, Alli closed her eyes when she found herself still shivering from the sensations that had gripped her the night before. She barely had been able to sleep, so instead she had decided to get up and think. However, she found that all she could do was mentally replay every single detail of being in Mark's arms.

An undefined ache still throbbed between her legs, and all during the night while trying to sleep she had shifted positions in an attempt to ease it. Whenever she had closed her eyes she had felt the pulsing heat from his erection pressed so intimately against her while he kissed her in a way that had melted her insides.

"This isn't good," she said softly with a sigh as she leaned back on the bench. She loved Mark but she wasn't sure she was ready for the degree of passion that he invoked.

Like his toe-curling kiss, for instance.

And although he had definitely left a lasting impression on her, she was convinced that she hadn't left any on him except possibly the question why a twenty-five-year-old woman knew absolutely nothing about the pleasures that men and women shared. He had even gone so far to admit that kissing her had been a mistake. But she didn't see things that way. What had been a mistake to him had been pure enjoyment to her.

Did he also see her being here as a mistake? Did he feel there was no way she could stay on as Erika's nanny since it was obvious that her presence was causing problems? What if he intended to take it further and ask her to quit her job as his assistant as well, since their employer-employee relationship had been breached? Panic tightened her throat. She couldn't lose her job now when Kara was depending so much on her.

Heaving a troubled sigh, she rose and walked back over to the bed. Feeling exhausted from lack of sleep, she decided to close her eyes and try to rest a while before Erika awakened for breakfast.

The last thing Alli wanted was to see Mark this morning, but she knew that was something she would not be able to avoid.

* * *

"Da-da. Eat."

Alli snapped her eyes open when the sound of Erika's voice seemed so close to her ear. She quickly turned over and remembered the monitor that Mark had installed in her room the day before. She smiled. Evidently Erika was awake and hungry.

Quickly getting out of bed, Alli slipped into her robe and, after tightening the belt securely around her waist, she opened her bedroom door only to collide with the solid wall of a male's chest.

"Oops."

"Sorry."

Mark caught her when she nearly lost her balance and the sensations she had been fighting all night intensified with his touch. As soon as he released her, she took a step back. "Thanks. I heard Erika."

He nodded. "So did I."

Alli noticed that his chin was covered with shaving cream, which meant he had been about to shave. She also noticed—although she wished she hadn't, but there was no way to avoid it—that he was bare-chested. The only thing covering his body was a pair of jeans and the towel wrapped around his neck. The top button of his jeans was undone and the dark mass of hair on his chest went down toward his abdomen and disappeared beneath the waist of his jeans. The one word that immediately came to Alli's mind was *sexy*.

When he leaned back against the wall and grinned, she frowned in confusion and wondered if he knew what she'd been thinking. "What's so funny?" she asked when he continued to grin.

"This," he said before reaching out and touching her cheek. He held up his finger.

"Oh," she said when she saw the shaving cream. She lifted a corner of her robe to wipe it off but he stopped her.

"No, let me."

Before she could stop him, he used his towel to wipe off her cheek. His touch was gentle and soft and the towel held his manly scent. She tried averting her gaze but found herself meeting his anyway. When she locked on the hazel eyes staring at her, she gulped, almost losing her breath. The heat that flared between them was instantaneous, absolute, blinding. And when he slid his gaze to her mouth, she had enough sense to know that she was in big trouble.

Deciding to head it off, she took another step back. "I need to go check on Erika."

He nodded and took a step back as well while placing the towel back around his neck. "We need to talk later, Alli."

She sighed deeply. "Yes...I know."

"But first I need to apologize about last night."

Stunned that he was placing the blame all on himself, she could only stare at him for a moment before finding her voice to say, "And I need to apologize as well."

He lifted an eyebrow. "For what?"

She shrugged. "For whatever you're apologizing for and for the fact that you evidently found me lacking."

Mark frowned. Apparently exhaustion was impairing his hearing. There was no way she could have said anything about him finding her lacking...was there? He leaned forward. "Lacking?"

"Yes." And without saying another word, she spun around and quickly entered the baby's room.

Totally stunned, he watched as Erika's door closed behind Alli. Seconds later he threw up his hand. *He found her lacking?* Where in the hell did she get a crazy idea like that? The last thing he thought was that she was lacking in anything. If the truth was known, he was convinced that she had an overabundance of everything, especially sensuality and passion. And he had a good mind to follow her into Erika's room to tell her that.

Okay, he quickly decided, now was not a good time to have that sort of a discussion with her. He needed time to think and he'd already told her that they needed to talk. He realized that they needed to do more than just talk. He definitely needed to straighten her out on a few things.

"Ah, just look at you," Alli whispered to Erika after putting the finishing touches on her hair. "Your uncle won't even recognize you."

Alli sighed. She'd had a lot of time to think while getting Erika dressed. Mark was right, they needed to talk. After what had happened last night and if he was uncomfortable with her being here, then she definitely would leave once he found someone to take her place. The same held true with the studio. If he felt their kiss had left it impossible for them to work together, then she would resign. It would be that simple.

She shook her head. She was fooling herself if she thought anything involving Mark Hartman was simple. But then she had known that living under the same roof with him wouldn't be easy given her feelings for him.

She inhaled a calming breath. Maybe it was time that she realized that nothing could, or would, ever develop between her and Mark. She could now admit that for the past two years she'd been waiting for a fairy tale to happen to her. A part of her had actually wanted to believe that one day she would walk into Hartman's Self-Defense Studio and Mark would see her with different eyes and realize she was capable of being more than just his dependable and efficient administrative assistant.

Well, okay, he had admitted that he thought she was beautiful. But she'd heard from several sources that men thought most women were beautiful; especially women they were interested in sleeping with. But now that Mark realized she couldn't kiss worth a damn and lacked the skills to pleasure a man, she was quite certain that any interest he might have had had died a sudden death.

And maybe it was for the best. If nothing else, her father's actions should have taught her that most men didn't deserve a woman's heart. All she had to do was remember the pain Arthur Lind had caused her mother to know that was true. In addition to that, Mark had told her yesterday he didn't want children. She, on the other hand, had made it pretty clear that she wanted several, which meant the things they wanted or didn't want out of life were vastly different.

At least with things ending this way she saved the humiliation of him finding out that she was in love with him. This way she could move on, concentrate on helping Kara finish college and then continue to live a peaceful existence for the rest of her life. It was time she began being practical and levelheaded.

Picking Erika up off the dressing table, Alli left the bedroom accepting the fact that handsome millionaires didn't fall in love with plain old regular folk like herself and it was time she got rid of any foolish romantic notions that such a thing was possible.

Mark could not stop staring the moment he walked into the kitchen. Both Erika and Alli looked different. It was quite obvious that Alli had taken the time to fix Erika's hair another way but the difference in Alli's appearance was a bit more startling.

She was wearing jeans.

Forget about the western shirt she also had on; his concentration was on her jeans and just how good she looked in them. He always thought she looked good wearing pants, but nothing—and he meant nothing— compared to her wearing jeans. Maybe it would not have been obvious if, when he had walked in the room, she hadn't been leaning over while searching inside the refrigerator.

Transfixed, he watched her move around his kitchen, unaware that he was watching her. Everything was shapely about her, lushly so, and the way the jeans fit her butt had him swallowing hard. And that wasn't the only thing that was feeling hard. He could actually feel his blood heat up, shooting hot fluid through all parts of his body, especially one particular stop. He shifted his position when he felt his erection strain against the zipper of his own jeans.

He couldn't help wondering how on earth he and Alli would maintain an employer-employee relationship now. Kissing her was bad enough, but having lustful thoughts about her was worse. Oh, as he had told her last night, he had wanted her for two years, yet had managed to keep his desire in check. But that was before he had tasted her and knew just how sweet and delicious she was. Now he would be hard-pressed to call her into his office without wanting to have his way with her on his desk.

"Da-da!"

Erika's outburst made Alli swing around, her gaze meeting his. Damn. He'd been caught staring. And when she reached up to get something out of his kitchen cabinet, causing the cotton shirt she was wearing to stretch tight across her breasts, he almost swallowed his tongue.

"I didn't hear you come in," Alli said in a breathless whisper that didn't help the erotic thoughts flowing through his head.

"Sorry, didn't mean to startle you," he said and walked over to where Erika was sitting in the high chair. The little girl automatically reached for him. "Da-da."

"Mark," he tried correcting her as he picked her up. He looked forward to the day when she would understand who he was and his role in her life. When she merely giggled and said, "Da-da," again, he shook his head. He studied the way her hair was styled and smiled. He liked it.

He glanced up to find Alli watching him, evidently waiting to hear his opinion. "I guess braiding her hair is better since it was getting all tangled. She was beginning to make a fuss whenever I combed it."

Alli nodded. "Yes, it will be more manageable this way." She turned back around to the stove. "Would you like something for breakfast? I'm fixing pancakes, eggs and bacon."

Mark wished she hadn't turned around, giving him

a view of her delectable backside. Her curves were out of this world and he couldn't help but appreciate just how snugly her jeans fit.

"Mark."

He blinked when she turned back and met his gaze. He had been caught staring again. "Ah, thanks for the offer but I have several appointments this morning. I had planned to come back here for lunch but I need to go out to the Windcroft horse ranch and talk to Nita."

Alli nodded. "The Texas Cattlemen are finally taking her seriously?"

Mark placed Erika on his shoulder while he leaned against the counter. He lifted an eyebrow. "You know about what she claims is going on over there at her farm?"

Alli shrugged. "I know what she's told me, and I have no reason not to believe her. I've known Nita a long time, every since Kara was small and Nita gave her riding lessons. There's no way she would make that stuff up."

Mark nodded as he returned Erika to the high chair. It was apparent that Alli had an idea that the Texas Cattleman's Club did more for the community than hosting fund-raisers, but he wasn't at liberty to disclose everything they did and felt the best thing to do would be to change the subject.

"How is your sister doing at college?" He watched as a frown puckered Alli's forehead.

"She was doing just fine until a few days ago when she met this guy at the library.

Mark heard the concern in her voice. "Is something wrong with her meeting guys?"

Alli's gaze narrowed. "She's at college to get a higher education, Mark, not to meet boys. She'll have plenty of time for a social life after she finishes school. Right now that's the main thing I want her to focus on. She's been making the dean's list every semester and I want her to continue to do so."

Mark nodded, wondering if perhaps Alli was expecting too much from her sister, but he decided it wasn't his business to mention that fact. Alli had begun working for him the summer before Kara had started college and he had met Kara several times when she had dropped by the studio to visit with Alli. Kara was a beautiful teenager who, in his book, was a younger version of Alli. Kara had been valedictorian of her senior class and her manners had been exemplary, which was a pretty darn good indication that Alli had done a great job raising her.

One of the reasons he had offered Alli so much money to work for him was that he'd heard about the extra expenses she would be putting out to assist her sister.

"I'll be at the studio if you need to reach me," he said, grabbing his hat off the rack. "You also know my mobile number."

"You haven't forgotten that I have class tonight have you, Mark?"

He dug into his pocket for the keys to his truck. "No, I haven't forgotten. I'll be home for dinner. Mrs. Sanders should be here around noon. If she asks, please tell her that I'd like to have some of her fried chicken, mash potatoes and gravy. She makes the best."

Alli smiled. "All right, I'll tell her."

Mark looked down at Erika and lightly pinched her cheek, making her squeal with laughter. "See you later, kid." He then looked at Alli and forced the thought from his mind of how much he wanted to walk across the room and kiss her goodbye. "I'll see you later, too," he said then headed for the door."

"Will we have our talk when you come home later?"

He stopped, turned around and met her gaze. "Yes, we'll talk then."

"So you're the new nanny?"

Alli smiled at the older woman who had shown up precisely at noon just as Mark had said she would. Erika had been fed lunch and was taking a nap, and Alli decided to take that time to do the baby's laundry. She was sitting at the kitchen table folding clothes while keeping the older woman company.

"Yes, but only on a temporary basis. I work as Mark's administrative assistant at the studio. He needed someone to fill in here and asked me to do it for a while."

The older woman shook her head as she tossed chicken in the bag to be floured. "I'm glad. Someone needed to help that boy with the baby."

Alli lifted an eyebrow, remembering what Mark had told her. "But you wouldn't," she decided to point out to the older woman.

Still shaking her head, Mrs. Sanders smiled over at her. "No. I had my reasons and they went deeper than what I told Mark. I felt he needed time to bond with his niece. When he brought her home he was a nervous wreck. Had I pitched in and helped, he would have depended on me and would have practically ignored that child. But I saw what was needed."

Alli leaned back in her chair. "And what was needed?"

"Time for him to get to know the baby, to remember

who she was and why she was here, to figure out things about her care on his own."

The older woman paused to peer into a pot that was cooking on the stove. In addition to making the dishes Mark had requested, she had decided to cook a huge pot of vegetable soup. She turned and met Alli's gaze. "Erika was such a precious thing when she first got here, but like most babies she was a little fidgety, crying all the time and whimpering. Mark didn't know how to do anything, not even change a diaper. I taught him the basics and told him the rest would come naturally. He'd learn as he went along. He caught on quick and is doing a wonderful job with her."

Alli nodded. She had to agree with that. "Have you known Mark long?" she asked as the woman began peeling potatoes.

"Practically all his life. I came to work for his pa off and on after his mother died. Mark was only seven at the time and Matt was five. Losing their mother was like losing their best friend. Carolina Hartman was a fine woman and to this day I never knew what she saw in Nathaniel. He was cold and heartless. All he ever cared about was this land and the oil that was on it. He wouldn't show affection of any kind, claimed it was a sign of weakness and punished his sons if they ever slipped and showed such an emotion in front of others. I remember Mark and Matt going to bed plenty of nights without supper after their mother died."

She joined Alli at the table. "Matt got punished all the time since he was so much like his mother he couldn't help it. Mark, on the other hand, learned to roll with the flow and did what the old man wanted so he wouldn't get into trouble. Hell knew no fury like Nathaniel Hartman's temper. That's the reason both Mark and Matt got the hell out of here as soon as they finished school. Mark left for the marines and two years later Matt left to attend college out west. Both swore they would never return to Royal while the old man was living and they kept their word. The only time they came back was for the funeral to see their pa laid to rest. I was so happy for Mark when he told me that he had met someone and planned to marry. Then I was so sad when I heard what had happened to his wife and he was left all alone. Too bad they never had any children. Mark had told me at his father's funeral that he didn't ever plan to have any. And he was pretty adamant about it, too."

Alli who had just folded one of Erika's shirts, glanced up and met Mrs. Sanders's gaze. "Why do you think he is so unyielding about it?"

The woman shook her head sadly. "Mark thinks he will grow up to be cold and heartless like his pa. Of course I don't believe it, which is why I wanted him to play a big part in Erika's care, just to prove him wrong. He needs to see that he's nothing like his old man. I'd watched him with that baby and he's given her so much love, affection and attention that at times I don't think he realizes that he's doing it."

Alli had to agree, thinking of him playfully tweaking Erika's cheek before he left. "It's sad that Mr. Hartman treated his sons that way. I remember hearing about it from my mom when I was younger and—"

"Your mom?" Mrs. Sanders asked with her bushy eyebrows arched.

"Yes, my mother used to do the ironing for Mr. Hartman years ago."

Rearing back, Mrs. Sanders sat in silence for a moment while staring at Alli, as if she were trying to make a connection to her last name as well as to her features. Then Mrs. Sanders's eyes lit up. "You're Mildred Lind's daughter?"

"Yes." Alli was surprised the woman would remember her mother.

The older woman laughed as she stood and walked over to the sink. "Well, I'll be. Now isn't it a small world? I knew your mother. We attended the same church for a while when she first married your father. My husband and I moved away for a few years. When we returned, instead of moving back to the city, we bought us a piece of property in the country since we needed a bigger spread to raise our kids."

She met Alli's gaze and regretfully shook her head. "I heard your mother had passed some years ago and I was sorry to hear about it. She was a good woman and a hard worker."

"Thank you." Alli paused, feeling a moment of unease when she wondered if Mrs. Sanders would bring up the incident involving her father at the time of her mother's death. News had gotten around about it when it had occurred eight years ago. It wasn't something most people would forget; at least she knew she never would.

Arthur Lind, who had deserted his wife and daughters years before, had shown up on the day of the funeral anticipating that he would inherit the house his wife had purchased without him. He actually had gotten ticked when he'd discovered she had willed it to her daughters.

He had filed a lawsuit claiming since he and his wife had never divorced, he deserved at least half of whatever assets she had accumulated.

Luckily for Alli and Kara, by the time the judge ordered her father to pay the back child-support payments he owed her and Kara, the amount was well over the equity he felt he was due from the house. In fact, he was ordered to pay an additional five thousand dollars, which he never did, and neither Alli nor Kara had heard from him again.

"You have no reason to thank me since I'm speaking the truth," Mrs. Sanders said as she resumed peeling the potatoes and glanced up for only a second. "How's your baby sister doing?"

Since it seemed that the older woman already had had a glimpse into her past, Alli spent the next ten minutes telling her how Kara had adjusted over the years and how well she was doing with her studies at college. Inwardly, she hoped her sister continued to do so. They hadn't talked since Kara had told her about her upcoming date for this weekend. Kara had dated some in high school but had never taken any of the guys seriously. But there had been something in her voice when she'd told Alli about the library guy that Alli had never heard before whenever the two of them had any discussions about the opposite sex.

"Something smells good in here."

Upon hearing Mark's voice, Alli whipped her head around and stared at him in surprise. She hadn't expected to see him until dinnertime. She took a deep breath and slowly exhaled. Seeing him again was turning her insides to mush. She may not have experienced the pleasures a man and a woman shared but being around Mark had her body yearning to do so. The memory of their kiss just wouldn't leave her alone.

He must have read the questions lodged in her eyes and said, "My last appointment canceled so I thought I'd drop by to see how things were going."

Before Alli could open her mouth to respond, Mrs. Sanders replied as she checked on the food she was cooking, "Things are going fine. Erika is sleeping, and Alli and I were taking the time to get to know each other."

"Hmm, you don't say?"

Alli decided not to say anything. Instead, she went about folding the last piece of Erika's laundry. She glanced up, however, when Mark came to stand beside the table.

"Do you think Erika will be sleeping for a while?" he asked.

Alli shrugged as she held his gaze. "It's hard to say. She's been sleeping for half an hour. I'd think she'll have another hour or so to go. Why?"

"I came by to see if the two of you wanted to take the ride with me over to Nita Windcroft's place."

"Oh."

"You two can go on. I'll keep an eye on Erika."

Alli stared at the older woman, surprised at her offer. Evidently Mark was surprised as well and said, "I thought you didn't take care of babies."

Mrs. Sanders flapped her hand before she lifted the lid of her pot. "I don't. But Erika is sleeping and chances are she'll stay that way for a while and if not, then I'll make an exception and handle things. No big deal."

"B-but, I—I'm sure he wanted Erika to go, too. This would have been a good outing for her," Alli sputtered, not sure she was ready to be alone with Mark. That would give them the perfect time for the talk they needed to have; something she wasn't looking forward to.

Leaning against the sink, Mrs. Sanders gazed at both her and Mark. "Well, Erika can't go because she's sleeping and I doubt you'd want to wake her. She's a fuss box if she doesn't get her rest." Frowning, the woman then dipped her chin as she stared at Mark. "Besides, I got the feeling that Mark just wanted some company."

Alli stole a quick glance at Mark. He was shaking his head, smiling while holding Mrs. Sanders's gaze, as if he knew what she was up to. Evidently there was a private joke going on that Alli wasn't privy to.

Mark then turned and met Alli's gaze. "Yes, I'd love the company if you'd like to go with me, Alli."

Inhaling a calming breath, Alli silently told herself that Mark was just being kind in asking her to go. The smart thing to do would be to turn down his offer. But then, as much as she wasn't looking forward to it, they needed to talk, and putting things off wouldn't help matters.

"Okay, I just need to put these things away and grab my jacket." She stood and, without looking at either him or Mrs. Sanders, walked out of the kitchen.

Alli took the time to do more than grab her jacket. She brushed her hair and applied some lip gloss. She also changed blouses since Erika accidentally had spilled some syrup on it at breakfast.

Moments later, she stared at her reflection in the mirror, deciding that she looked decent. She sucked in a deep breath as she left the bedroom and decided to quickly check on Erika. Alli stopped dead in her tracks when she found Mark in the room standing over the crib staring down at the sleeping baby.

Alli wanted to give him a private moment with his niece. She was quietly backing out of the room, more than certain he hadn't heard her, when he turned his head and met her gaze.

She opened her mouth to apologize for the untimely intrusion when he placed a finger to his lips and beckoned for them to step outside the room. After following her into the hall, he closed the door behind them.

"Sorry, I thought I'd check on her before we left," Alli said softly, trying not to notice how close together they were standing. She could see the irises of his hazel eyes as well as smell the masculine scent of the cologne he wore.

He smiled in understanding. "I thought I'd check on her, too. For some reason I like watching her sleep. She seems so at peace," he murmured.

Alli returned his smile. Earlier today she had thought the same thing. "She's that way when she's awake as well. Erika is a happy baby."

Mark lifted an eyebrow. "You really think so?"

Alli chuckled. "Yes. She has such a good temperament and is a joy to take care of."

Mark couldn't help but be pleased at what Alli had said. "Her father was that way. No matter how bad things were around here, nothing could break Matt's spirit, although the old man tried. My brother was always able to look on the bright side."

Alli felt a tugging at her heart. She couldn't help but recall the conversation she'd had with Mrs. Sanders and could only imagine Mark and his brother as young boys dealing with a father who thought it was wrong for him or his sons to show emotions.

"Ready to go?"

Mark's question jarred her out of her reverie. She stared at him for a moment and then asked, "I know you're visiting Nita on Texas Cattleman's Club business. Are you sure you want me to come along?"

He nodded his head. "Yes, I'm sure. Besides, this will give us time to talk."

Alli nodded. That's what she'd been afraid of.

Five

Mark glanced over at Alli as they walked out to his truck, not able to suppress his full awareness of her. He could feel her nervous tension and wondered if it was because of him.

He knew that kissing her had been a mistake, although, heaven help him, he wanted to do it again. The desire for her wouldn't go away. It was as if the lust that had been building and accumulating for two years was demanding to break free. They had crossed the boundary of what was acceptable between an employer and his employee and he couldn't help wondering what she thought about it. His actions last night had put him at risk of losing the best assistant he'd ever had.

But as much as he tried, he could not ignore her presence. He had dated some since his return to Royal but never had he let any woman get close to him. In fact, other than Erika, Mrs. Sanders, Christine Travers, the interior decorator and the other piss-poor nannies he'd hired, no other female had been allowed across the threshold in his home.

He was suddenly pulled from his thoughts when, to avoid coming into contact with the branch of a shrub, Alli moved closer to him and innocently touched her arm to his. He stiffened when a jolt of awareness shot through him. Just being around her was murder on his self-control.

How in the world could she think that she was lacking in anything? he wondered again. Although he could tell she wasn't an experienced kisser, that hadn't had any bearing on how she had made him feel. In fact, he had found her inexperience totally refreshing and unique. There weren't too many twenty-five-year-olds who hadn't been in and out of numerous affairs. After thinking about it most of the day, he realized that during the two years Alli had worked for him, he'd never known her to go out on a date, not that he was privy to everything there was to know about her personal life and how she spent her free time.

Hell, for all he knew she could have had a boyfriend, several of them. How did he know for sure that she didn't have one now? She was a beautiful woman, a real head-turner no matter where she went, so it was possible she *was* seeing someone. For some reason, he was disturbed at the thought that there might be a special man in her life, although he had no right to feel that way.

He sighed deeply. Instead of his mind being focused on Alli and whether or not she was involved with someone, he should be concentrating on his meeting with Nita Windcroft.

But he knew he couldn't put it off any longer. He and Alli needed to talk.

Mark and Alli rode for about four miles before either one of them spoke.

"It won't be much farther now," Mark said, glancing over at her.

"Yes, I know." Alli turned from looking out the window and glanced over at him, barely seeing his eyes because of the wide brim of his Stetson. "You said that we would talk." She had decided that if she needed to look for other employment, the sooner she did so, the better.

"Yes, I did." He glanced back over at her again. "About last night. I think you misunderstood the reason I was apologizing."

She lifted an eyebrow. "Did I?"

He gave her a lazy smile. "Yes, I think you did."

She took a deep breath, reminding herself that lately she and Mark weren't on the same wavelength, so she decided to let him do the explaining. "I don't understand what you're saying, Mark."

She blinked when she saw he was pulling to the side of the road, and once they were stopped, he turned off the engine of his truck. He turned in his seat to face her, tipping his hat back. In a way, Alli wished that he hadn't done that. Now she could see his eyes and the intensity she saw in them made her breath catch.

"The reason I apologized, Alli, was because I'm the one who initiated the kiss and I was out of line to do so. When I said that we made a mistake, what I meant was that the kiss should not have happened. I told you that I wasn't ready to become involved with anyone. But last night I gave into a weakness I've been fighting for two years."

Alli blinked in surprise. "Two years?"

He smiled warmly. "Yes, for two years. I've wanted to kiss you for a very long time and my apology had nothing to do with your lack of experience."

Alli wanted to believe what he was saying. "I wasn't sure since I haven't dated much. Over the years, even while I was in high school, taking care of Kara occupied most of my time and there wasn't time for dates."

There was no way she was going to tell him that once Kara had left for school she could have started dating, but by that time she had fallen in love with him and no other man had interested her.

"I don't want to become involved with you, Alli."

She pursed her lips and raised her chin. "And I don't want to become involved with you, either."

"Good. I'm glad we agree on that. Another kiss would be asking for trouble."

"I totally agree."

He leaned back in his seat. "If we were to kiss again it will be hard for us to go back to having a strictly professional relationship."

"I concur with that as well."

"We will be living together for a while and since we know what's the most sensible thing to do, which is the only thing that we can do, what do you suggest?" His gaze slid to her mouth. She saw it happen and her pulse quickened.

"I could leave here today and, if you want, I'll even quit my job at the studio."

"No. That's not what I want, Alli." Mark rubbed his hand down his face. He needed to rid her of the notion that he preferred she leave.

"I need you here, Alli, and when I find a nanny who I can depend on, I'll need you back at the studio. In no way am I suggesting that you stop working for me."

"Then what are you saying?"

His muscles tightened at the memory of what had happened to Patrice and the months of endless guilt he endured following her death. Never again would he set himself up for such heartbreak. The quicker he established some distance between Alison and him, the better things would be for both of them.

His eyes met hers. "What I'm trying to say is that I need to practice more self-control when it comes to you. But it won't be easy. I need your help. We both need to accept that we're attracted to each other. It's an attraction that will lead nowhere, since I don't ever intend to get serious about a woman again." He held her gaze intensely. "Do you understand what I'm trying to say, Alli?"

She nodded, fighting the tightness in her throat. He was telling her in a nice way that he didn't want her. Ever. "You want to keep things as they have been between us for the past two years, a strictly professional relationship. Is that what you want?"

Mark nodded. "Yes, that is exactly what I want."

"We're here," Mark said, glancing over at Alli. She hadn't said more than two words to him since they'd had their talk. More than once he had tried to strike up a conversation with her but in a polite yet distant way she had let him know she wasn't prone to chitchat. In fact, she was doing exactly what he'd asked her to do—establish a strictly professional relationship between them.

And already he didn't like it.

He glanced out of his truck's windshield and stared at the main house of the Windcrofts' Horse farm. The structure was very modern with a lot of tall windows and a stone facade. The primary stable was located close to the house and an older farmhouse—probably the original family dwelling—was set back in the distance. There were also four corrals, stallion pens as well as a training pen.

From his early days of living in Royal, Mark recalled that Will Windcroft's wife had died when his two daughters, Nita and Rose, were small children. The Windcroft girls were as different as day and night. It had always been Rose's dream to leave Royal and pursue a career in the big city. Nita never wanted to leave and had looked forward to continuing her father's horse-breeding farm. In recent years, as business had increased, she'd begun assuming a greater role in running things.

"I've always liked this place."

Mark jerked his head around. Alli had spoken without being prompted. It suddenly occurred to him how much he liked hearing her voice. Even while at the studio when she was going over reports, he would be more in tune to listening to her voice than concentrating on the subject they were discussing.

"My dad used to purchase his horses from Mr. Windcroft and I've always liked it here, too," he said. "You come here often?" he asked, wanting to keep her talking. Just because they had agreed to have a strictly business relationship was no reason they had to act like total strangers.

"Not as often as I'd like to. When I was a little girl, Mr. Windcroft taught me how to ride my first horse, and later when Nita took over the running of things, she taught Kara. Even now there are days on the weekend when I'll come and get one of their horses and ride for hours, although not as often as I used to."

Mark gave her an incredulous look. Though he knew most people in Royal could ride, he never gave it much thought that she could. For some reason, he could not imagine her sitting on the back of a horse. She seemed too prim and proper for that. "I have horses at my ranch. You're welcome to take one out whenever you want. John Collier is my foreman. He'll be glad to saddle one up for you."

She glanced at him as she brushed her hair back from her face. "Thanks."

Before he could say anything, she opened the truck's door and hopped out. He figured she was putting distance between them again. He inhaled deeply as he opened his own door. And for the second time he had to remind himself that he was getting just what he'd asked for.

She wasn't trying to be difficult, Alli tried convincing herself. What she was doing was trying to make the best of a difficult situation. Mark had made things pretty clear. In order to keep her job, she needed to keep her distance and he would keep his. Although it would be challenging with them living under the same roof, she intended to do it.

She smiled when she saw Jimmy, the Windcrofts' foreman, approaching. However, she tensed when she felt Mark's presence beside her. She hadn't wasted any time getting out of the truck because of the desperate need to catch her breath and gather her composure. She was sure Mark wasn't aware of it, but each and every time he looked at her for too long or got too close to her, her insides filled with heat. She walked away from him to meet Jimmy, needing desperately to escape his presence.

"Ms. Lind, how are you?" Jimmy greeted her, smiling brightly. "It's been a while since you've come out for a ride."

She returned the man's smile. "Yes, I've been pretty busy lately. How is everything going?"

Before Jimmy could respond, his gaze moved to Mark, who had joined them. "Jimmy, do you know Mark Hartman?" Alli asked. "He's here to talk to Nita."

The two men regarded each other as introductions were made and handshakes exchanged. "I don't think we've ever met, since I was hired on here after you left Royal years ago," Jimmy was saying. "You own the Hartman place, right?"

Mark smiled. "Yes, that's right."

"You have a mighty fine spread."

"Thanks. Is Nita around?"

"Yeah, she's out back near the stables with a few of the hands. I'll be glad to take you to her," Jimmy said. He then glanced over at Alli. "Are you coming, too, Ms. Lind?"

Alli shook her head. "No, I think I'll go inside and visit with Will and Jane. Is she in?"

Jimmy chuckled. "Now you know Jane isn't going any-place," he said of the Windcrofts' housekeeper. "In fact, there's a rumor floating around the farm that she's baking a ton of pies today, so you came to visit right in time."

"That's wonderful. I love Jane's pies," Alli said chuckling. She made a move to step past Mark and he reached out and touched her arm. Although she tried to remain unaffected, every part of her tingled from the contact.

"I'll see you again in a little while," he said huskily, the depth of his gaze holding hers.

She gave him a strained smile. "All right." And then she quickly walked off toward the main house.

When they reached the stables, Mark looked around. Several ranch hands were crowded around the training pen watching one of the hands break in a horse. The animal was a beauty. He was also mean and it was obvious that he intended to throw the rider. However, the rider was showing the animal that he wasn't going any-where. There was nothing like seeing man tame beast... or vice versa.

Fascinated, Mark walked to the corral and joined the onlookers. Everyone was cheering the rider on and, from the way the man was handling the horse, it appeared he was definitely up to the challenge, even with the horse not making it easy for him bucking all over the place.

The longer Mark watched, the more fascinated he became with the rider's skills. Moments later when it became evident the cowboy was the victorious one, a loud cheer went up. "What a way to go, Nita!" the crowd called out.

Mark blinked. "Nita?"

He stared at the rider who was getting off the horse and, when her feet touched the ground, she pulled off her hat, spilling a mass of black hair that she'd tucked underneath. She smiled and waved to the crowd.

"Damn." That was the only word Mark could think to say at that moment. How could he have forgotten that Nita Windcroft could outrace, out rope and outride just about any male?

He watched as the slim woman glanced his way after Jimmy said something to her. Without a hint of any smile on her face, she walked toward Mark. When she reached him, instinctively he held out his hand. She took it, although a deep, dark frown had settled on her face.

She met his gaze. "Hi, Mark. It's about time one of you guys decided to pay a visit."

Mark nodded. He knew she had expected them to drop everything and come running the first time she'd come to them claiming that the Devlins were causing mischief. "Any new developments, Nita?" he asked.

She placed her hands on her hips and glared at him. "Like poisoned feed, broken fences, cut lines, spooked horses and threatening notes aren't enough?"

Mark sighed deeply. The Texas Cattleman Club had seen the so-called threatening notes and thought they were too vague to actually take seriously, and although Nita had disagreed, there was no evidence that indicated the Devlins were involved. "Have you received another threatening note?"

"No."

"Then things have gotten back to calm around here?"

Nita narrowed her eyes. "For now but I'm not going to hold my breath it will last."

Mark nodded. "I'd like to take a look around."

"That's fine. I'm just glad to see you guys are finally taking me serious."

Mark sighed, choosing not to tell her it hadn't been decided if they were taking her seriously or not. "It might be a good idea if we have a list of names of anyone and everyone you do business with. It could come in handy later."

Nita nodded. "All right. It will take me a few moments to print it off the computer."

After Nita left, Mark checked out the other areas of her property, looking for anything that could give him a hint of who might be responsible for the activities going on at her place.

Mark had circled around the back of the stable when suddenly something lying on the ground near the barn caught his attention. He kneeled down for a closer look. Lying in the grass near a shrub was a syringe, the kind typically used in hospitals to give injections.

He sighed deeply. It was probably the same kind, or pretty similar, to the one used to kill Jonathan Devlin.

Six

"I'm leaving for class now, Mark."

Mark glanced up from the printout of names he'd gotten from Nita Windcroft to Alli as she walked into the room. Ever since their talk earlier that day, things had been strained between them. They had barely said two words to each other on the ride back from the Windcroft farm.

He glanced out the window. It was already dark and the thought of her going out alone at night bothered him. He remembered the incident with her car breaking down and stood to fish his car keys out of the pocket of his jeans. "Here, use my car."

Alli stared at the keys he held out to her. She then looked up with a puzzled expression on her face. "Why?"

"Because I rarely drive it since I mostly use the truck and it's in a lot better shape than yours."

Alli frowned. Well, of course his car was in better shape, for heaven's sake. Her car was eight years old and his brand new Maxima probably hadn't hit one hundred miles yet. Although what he said was true, she didn't appreciate him pointing out that fact. "Thanks for the offer but I prefer driving my own car."

From the expression on his face, she could tell he didn't like her response. "Why?" he asked.

She managed a smile when she said, "Because I just do."

Immediately she could tell he liked that response even worse. He crossed his arms over his chest. "I prefer that you take mine."

Her frown deepened. "Again thanks for the offer, Mark, but I prefer driving my own car."

She watched as he took a deep breath and glared at her. "You need a new car."

Again what he said was true but she resented him telling her that. "I plan to get a new one this weekend when Jake has the time to go with me to the dealership."

His dark eyebrows arched. "Jake?"

"Yes, Jake. Christine thought a man should go with me when I pick out a car since some salesmen have a tendency of taking advantage of female customers." She turned to leave.

"You could have asked me to go with you," Mark snapped angrily.

Alli stopped and turned around. She met his glare as calmly as she could and wondered just what his problem was. "No, I could not have asked you to go with me, Mark."

A confused look covered his face. "Why not?"

"It would not have been ethical. Jake is a friend. You're my employer. Good night." She then paused long enough to bend down to give Erika a kiss on the cheek before walking out the room.

With an agitation that he felt all the way down to his toes, Mark sat on the sofa across from the television as he flipped though several channels before muttering a curse and tossing the remote aside. He stood and began pacing the floor.

It was one of those rare nights that Erika had fallen asleep early, and although there were a number of things he could be doing, he could barely concentrate.

Alli had really ticked him off. The nerve of her asking Jake instead of him to go with her to pick out a car. Mark would have been glad to assist her in making a selection. Then for her to say she hadn't asked since he was her employer really grated on his nerves.

He was about to go into the kitchen for a beer when he heard a knock at the door. He glanced at the clock on the wall. Alli's class wouldn't be over for another hour and she had her own key. Fear gripped his gut. Was someone at the door to tell him something had happened to her? Had her car broken down by the side of the road and…

He inhaled deeply as he rushed to the window and looked out. He quickly let out a deep breath of relief when he saw it was Gavin's SUV out front. He had totally forgotten that he had called Gavin earlier and asked him to stop by.

He walked over to the door and opened it. "Evening, Sheriff." Mark was tall but Gavin O'Neal was taller, which was something Mark couldn't help but notice when the man walked into the house.

"Mark. Sorry it took so long for me to get here but I had to transport a prisoner to Midland. You indicated when you called that you may have found something out at the Windcrofts' place today."

"Yes," Mark said as he crossed the room to retrieve the bag he had placed in his desk drawer. "Like I told you, it's a syringe. I know syringes are used in the breeding of horses but this one is the kind used in hospitals for human injections."

Gavin took the clear plastic bag Mark handed him and studied the syringe inside of it. "Did you mention you had found this to Nita?"

Mark shook his head. "No, I didn't mention it to anyone. Luckily I was alone when I found it."

Gavin nodded. "Good. The last thing we need is word getting out and people speculating whether or not it's connected to Jonathan's murder since it's all around town that he was killed with some sort of lethal injection. The lab is closed tonight but I'll have it to them first thing in the morning. It shouldn't take long for them to analyze it and get back to us. I hope to have their report at our club meeting on Wednesday night."

"Here's a list of names of Nita's entire clientele, which includes anyone using her breeding services, those she's giving riding lessons to, as well as everyone who boards their horses in her stables."

Gavin let out a whistle as he accepted the pages from Mark. "It seems she does a lot of business."

"Yes, which is the main reason she wants us to do

something to stop what's going on. If word gets out that she's being harassed, she can start losing business. People will be afraid to patronize her."

"You have a point there," Gavin said, glancing down at his watch. "I hate to run but I need to get by the Royal Diner for a cup of coffee before they close."

Mark lifted an eyebrow knowing that a cup of coffee wasn't the only interest Gavin had at the diner. He tried hiding his smile when he said, "You're in luck, Sheriff. I just made a fresh pot and you're welcome to a cup if you like."

Gavin shot him a quick apologetic look, and then said, "Ah, sorry, no offense, I'm sure your coffee is decent but I like the diner's coffee better. Thanks for the offer though." He quickly headed for the door.

Mark chuckled as he locked the door behind Gavin, thinking that, whether or not Gavin realized it, he was definitely acting like a man smitten.

Alli opened the door and breezed through it still feeling elated. She had gotten an A on her paper tonight and she was thrilled. Professor Jones was a stickler for grades and she was trying hard to make it through the end of the semester without getting on his bad side the way a lot of the other students were doing.

Taking classes part-time was bad enough and she didn't envy her sister one bit with her full load, which was one of the main reasons she didn't want Kara to lose focus on her studies. The only good thing, Alli thought, about her own personal situation was that she could finally see a light at the end of the tunnel. Taking two classes for the next four semesters—even though it meant going to school year-round—and she could be graduating in December of next year.

"You're back."

Alli whirled around clutching her chest. Mark had practically scared the living daylights out of her. She watched as he straightened away from the wall and emerged out of the shadows to stand in front of her.

She met his gaze as she forced her heartbeat back to normal. "Yes, I'm back."

She stared at him. He was wearing a pair of blue silk pajamas and a matching bathrobe. "I didn't expect to see you," she said quickly as she tried not to stare, but she'd always thought that blue was his color. "I thought you'd be in bed."

"I was but my throat got dry and I decided to get up for a glass of water."

"Oh."

"And how was class?"

She wanted to say that her class was none of his business. But since Hartman's Self-Defense Studio's tuition-aid policy was paying a percentage of her college expenses, he did have a right to know how the investment was paying off. "Class was great tonight and I got an A on my paper," she said excitedly.

He smiled. "That's great."

"Thanks."

"You, Erika and I will have to celebrate."

Alli lifted an eyebrow. "Celebrate?"

"Yes. I think it's something worth celebrating. It's not easy to get an A on a paper in college these days."

"Yes, but—"

"Then it's settled. Erika and I usually eat at the

Royal Diner on Friday evenings and we invite you to join us."

Alli stared down at the floor as she thought about his invitation. She looked up and met his gaze. Her mouth tightened briefly. "How does dinner with you and Erika fall under the category of an employer-employee relationship?"

A smile touched the corners of Mark's lips. "That's easy enough to define," he said simply. "I've hired you to take care of my niece and as her nanny you'll be there enjoying a meal with us." He held her gaze for a moment, then he asked, "Does that suit you?"

Alli inhaled deeply. No, that didn't suit her, not after he had made it absolutely clear that he wanted distance between them. Having dinner with him tomorrow night was not keeping distance. "If I remember correctly we agreed that I would have Friday and Saturday evenings off," she said, reminding him of that fact.

He slanted her a glance that looked as if he might argue the point. Then he said, "You're right. I had forgotten about that. The three of us will have to celebrate some other time, perhaps."

"Perhaps. Now if you'll excuse me, I want to check on Erika before I go to bed."

Without giving him a chance to say anything else, she quickly walked out of the room.

Mark lay in bed and sucked in a sharp breath as soon as he heard the shower come on in the bedroom next to his. It didn't take much to visualize Alli undressing—first, taking off the dress she had worn to school, followed by her slip, bra and panties. Then stepping beneath the pounding spray of warm water as it cascaded over her body, soaking her face and running rivulets down her neck to flow over her breasts.

He further imagined that at some point she would grab hold of one of those bottles of shower gel that he had seen her unpack yesterday and dab an ample amount in the palms of her hands to rub generously over her body, starting with her flat stomach, then moving upward to her breasts, making circles around her nipples, coming back lower to massage her curves, before reaching down to her thighs and then the area between her legs and…

He bolted up, unable to handle the vision any longer. Why couldn't he follow her lead and accept what he himself had decreed regarding their relationship? *Strictly professional.* She had accepted his dictate and moved on. It seemed that he was the one who had issues. Such as with Jake going to the dealership with her to purchase a new car instead of Mark.

He dropped back down in bed thinking, *Fat chance of that happening!* She was his employee. He was the one who had given her the bonus for the down payment on the car. If anyone deserved to be there when she purchased a new vehicle, it was him. Satisfied he had reached that conclusion, he decided he would contact Jake tomorrow…on behalf of his employee. And what was the problem if she considered him a friend as well? A lot of bosses had friendly yet professional relationships with their staff.

Mark lay down, wondering why that thought hadn't occurred to him before. Probably because over the past two years he had been too busy fighting his attraction to her. What he should have been doing was getting to know her as a friend on a professional level. There was no law that said she couldn't be his assistant as well as his friend. It would definitely relieve some of the tension he felt when they worked together, and it would contribute to a more comfortable environment regardless of whether it was at his home or at the studio.

So, as far as he was concerned, there was no reason the two of them couldn't get better acquainted while she was staying in his house, as long as they established boundaries. And the first thing he had to do was get rid of any and all lustful thoughts about Alli that were plaguing him.

With that decision made, he felt a lot better and snuggled under the covers, pulling the pillow over his head. As sleep came down upon him, his earlier imaginings returned and invaded his unconscious mind.

It was the vision of Alli in the shower.

Alli stepped out of the shower and grabbed a towel to dry herself. She had been excited about her grade from Professor Jones until Mark had made the suggestion that she join him and Erika for dinner tomorrow night. There was no way she could do that and have people speculating that she had designs on her boss. She had loved him secretly for two years without anyone having a clue and she intended to keep things that way.

She knew after what he'd said on their way over to the Windcrofts' place that nothing would ever develop between them. He saw her as his employee and nothing more. At least she would have memories of the one and only time they'd kissed—how he'd held her in his arms, how his mouth had moved over hers and how her mouth had parted instinctively when he had inserted his tongue. And when he had deepened the kiss, taken her mouth with a skill and a mastery she hadn't known existed, she had felt sensations and emotions unlike any she'd had before. And now, although she was still damp from her shower, she could feel heat flow through her belly and settle right smack between her thighs.

She sighed so deeply it was almost a moan deep in her throat. She would always remember the taste of him, a taste she was dying to sample again, but knew there was no way that she ever would.

She would have to be satisfied with her memories.

Seven

Mark walked into the kitchen the next morning in a much better mood than he'd been in the night before. Immediately his eyes lit on Alli. She was standing in front of the high chair, showing Erika how to hold her spoon properly, and was dressed in a T-shirt that advertised Hartman's Self-Defense Studio and a pair of black walking shorts.

He shook his head and smiled. Even now, she was trying to keep her attire modest and professional. He had discovered a long time ago that it didn't matter what type of clothing Alison Lind placed on her body—she would still look delectable. The red-and-white T-shirt was tucked inside her shorts and emphasized her small waist and curvy hips. And her shorts showed enough of her long, slender legs to remind him of the visions that had taken over his dreams last night. In all his twenty-eight years, he had never dreamed about a woman taking a bath.

His dream had alternated with visions of her bath and of him kissing her. He had kissed her so much that she had begged him to make love to her. And he'd been about to do just that when his alarm had gone off.

Sighing deeply, he forced his gaze from Alli to his niece. Erika seemed to be enjoying Alli's instructions. He couldn't help but notice how his niece was dressed. Since Alli's arrival two days ago, Erika's hair was combed differently, in a cute little style, and she wore ribbons and bows to coordinate with whatever outfit she had on that day, not to mention the matching stocks.

As he leaned against the wall, he had to admit that the way Erika was dressed was just one of many noticeable changes Alli had made in less than seventy-two hours. His niece seemed to smile even more. She ate home-cooked oatmeal instead of the instant kind, and Alli had no problems cooking a full-course breakfast whenever his niece muttered the word *egg*.

Then there was the scent that always emitted from Alli's bedroom whenever he passed it. It was a feminine scent. A woman's scent. More than once he had paused in the hallway outside her door to get his bearings and to remind himself that a woman was now in residence…as if he really needed reminding. There was no way he could forget that Alli was in his house.

"Da-da!"

He couldn't help but smile when two pairs of eyes lit on him. From Alli's expression it was plain that she was surprised to see him. Had she forgotten that he lived here? "Good morning," he said coming into the room.

"Good morning. I thought you were gone," Alli said still eyeing him strangely. "When I got up and looked out the window I saw your truck driving away."

He nodded, now understanding her confusion. "John is using my truck to pick up supplies. His is in the shop getting repaired."

"Oh." She then turned her attention back to Erika. He felt dismissed and ignored when she began talking to Erika and telling her how good oatmeal was for her.

He walked across the room and his niece's attention switched from Alli to him and she extended her arms for him to pick her up. "Da-da."

He gently tweaked her cheek, then said, "No, sweetheart, I'm Mark. And Alli needs to feed you so you can grow up to be big, strong and healthy like your daddy was."

"She won't understand the name thing until she gets a little older, Mark," Alli said, standing beside him. He glanced at her. Instead of looking back at him, she kept her gaze focused on Erika, but he didn't miss the guarded look on Alli's face, as if she were protecting herself from something. He couldn't help wondering just what that something was.

She walked toward the sink. "I'm taking Erika with me on an outing today," she said over her shoulder.

"Oh? Where are you ladies going?"

She turned around. The guarded look had been replaced with a bright smile. "Car shopping. I thought I'd take the time to look around today so that when Jake meets with me tomorrow I'll have an idea of the type of vehicle I want."

He nodded. "That's a good idea, however there's a problem with that."

THE EDITOR'S "THANK YOU" FREE GIFTS INCLUDE:

▶ Two BRAND-NEW Harlequin® Next™ Novels

▶ An exciting surprise gift

YES! I have placed my Editor's "thank you" Free Gifts seal in the space provided at right. Please send me 2 FREE books, and my FREE Mystery Gift. I understand that I am under no obligation to purchase anything further, as explained on the back and opposite page.

PLACE
FREE GIFTS
SEAL
HERE

▶ DETACH AND MAIL CARD TODAY! ▶

356 HDL D74J   156 HDL D72U

FIRST NAME	LAST NAME

ADDRESS

APT.#	CITY

STATE/PROV.	ZIP/POSTAL CODE

Thank You!

(HN-PAS-11/05)

The Reader Service — Here's How It Works:

Accepting your 2 free books and gift places you under no obligation to buy anything. You may keep the books and gift and return the shipping statement marked "cancel." If you do not cancel, about a month later we'll send you 3 additional books and bill you just $3.99 each in the U.S., or $4.74 each in Canada, plus 25¢ shipping & handling per book and applicable taxes if any.* That's the complete price and — compared to cover prices of $5.50 each in the U.S. and $6.50 each in Canada — it's quite a bargain! You may cancel at any time, but if you choose to continue, every month we'll send you 3 more books, which you may either purchase at the discount price or return to us and cancel your subscription.

*Terms and prices subject to change without notice. Sales tax applicable in N.Y. Canadian residents will be charged applicable provincial taxes and GST.

If offer card is missing write to: The Reader Service, 3010 Walden Ave., P.O. Box 1867, Buffalo, NY 14240-1867

BUSINESS REPLY MAIL
FIRST-CLASS MAIL   PERMIT NO. 717-003   BUFFALO, NY

POSTAGE WILL BE PAID BY ADDRESSEE

THE READER SERVICE
3010 WALDEN AVE
PO BOX 1867
BUFFALO NY 14240-9952

NO POSTAGE
NECESSARY
IF MAILED
IN THE
UNITED STATES

She lifted an eyebrow. "What?"

"I spoke to Jake earlier this morning about TCC business, and he mentioned all the things he has going on this weekend. It seems that someone has pulled up his campaign signs and he and his workers are going to be busy tomorrow going around town replacing them."

Seeing her disappointed look, he added, "I told him you would understand and that since I was free tomorrow I'd be glad to go with you."

"But, but I thought that—"

"For me to go car shopping with you is perfectly fine," he rushed on to assure her. "No matter what, we still need to maintain a friendly working relationship, right?"

"Yes, but—"

"Then it's settled. I'll go with you tomorrow and I don't want you to worry about a thing. All right?"

Reluctantly she nodded.

"Good. Now I hope you ladies enjoy your day."

He smiled as he quickly walked out of the kitchen, not giving her the chance to say anything.

Mark looked at the sporty SUV and then at Alli. He raised an eyebrow. "Are you sure this is the vehicle you want?"

She smiled brightly. "Yes, I'm sure. Erika and I saw it yesterday and the man was nice enough to let me give it a test drive and I love it. I know it doesn't look like me but this is what I want."

She was right. It didn't look like her. He hadn't pegged her as the sports-utility-vehicle type. She looked like someone who would drive a car similar to the one she had now—a low-key four-door sedan. The vehicle she had selected, with its leather seats, sunroof, state-of-the-art sound system, just to name a few of the features, was definitely sporty.

Sighing, he turned to the salesman who'd been waiting patiently. "This is the one she'll take. And I want you to work up the best deal along with the best payment terms. Understand?"

The man smiled eagerly. "Yes, Mr. Hartman. Mr. Cross said you were a personal friend of his and to make sure we take care of you right."

Mark nodded. He and Stan Cross had gone to high school together and Mark had been glad when Alli had mentioned the vehicle she wanted was at this particular dealership. "Now we have two reasons to celebrate and I would like to invite you to dine with me and Erika at the Royal Diner."

"I thought you and Erika ate at the Royal Diner yesterday," she said, placing Erika back into the stroller. Alli had stayed at her own house last night to do some more packing, and had been glad to see Erika when she had arrived at the ranch this morning. And although she didn't want to admit it, she had been glad to see Mark as well.

"No matter how often you eat there, the food is always good," Mark said grinning. "So how about it? After spending so much fun time with you, I believe Erika is beginning to peg me as a bore. Whenever I look after her, she goes to bed early."

Alli held his gaze and her pulse quickened at the teasing warmth she saw in his hazel eyes. She would love go to out to eat with him and Erika but she didn't want to cause problems regarding their working relationship. "Are you sure it will be okay if we were to go to dinner together?"

Mark nodded. A part of him regretted he'd ever had that conversation with her. "Yes, I'm sure. So how about if we finalize the paperwork for your new vehicle and then we can meet up at the diner?"

Alli smiled. "All right."

The tinkle of the little gold bell that hung over the entrance door of the Royal Diner signaled Alli's arrival. The diner was your typical family café that didn't serve alcoholic beverages. The waitresses wore pink short-sleeve polyester dresses with well-above-the-knee hems and tailored collars and small white aprons.

The diner wasn't the best-looking place in town, with its worn and cracked dull-gray linoleum floor and the faded red plastic booth seats, as well as the scratched chrome strips that edged the tabletops, but the food—thanks to a cook by the name of Manny Reno—was mouthwateringly delicious.

Alli could almost smell his famous coconut-cream pie the moment she walked through the door. She glanced around and saw Mark waving to get her attention. She couldn't help but grin when she saw Erika following her uncle's lead and waving as well. Alli made her way around the long Formica counter toward the booth in the back.

The jukebox was playing a Ray Charles tune and, as expected, the diner was packed. It seemed that regardless of whether you were rich or poor, the Royal Diner was the place to be on Saturday evening and Manny's sinfully juicy hamburgers and coconut-cream pie were the hot items on the menu.

As Alli glanced across the room at Mark, she thought he was hot off the menu. She may not know a lot about the intimacies men and women shared, but she could recognize sexual tension and it seemed that whenever the two of them were together the air was full of it.

Every time she saw him, no matter the time or the place, she was reminded of their kiss, the feel of his mouth on hers, and how she had returned the kiss with everything she had, becoming rocked by sensations that still flooded her.

And she was frightened by them.

She didn't want to think about what might happen if those sensations continued to consume her. Now that she and Mark had had their talk, she wanted to do the right thing, which meant she needed to stop thinking about the one time they had made a mistake, as he'd put it, and crossed over boundaries that they shouldn't have.

Mark stood when she reached the booth. "Sorry, I'm late but I wanted to cruise awhile and try out everything," she said taking the seat across from him. Erika was sitting in a toddler seat next to Mark.

Mark sat back down and grinned. "And how does it drive?"

She gave him a cheeky smile. "Like a charm. I love it and it's so easy to maneuver. I can't wait for Kara to see it."

He smiled at her. "When will she be home?"

"I'm hoping next weekend. She's carrying a full load this semester and has a lot of studying to do." A few moments later she said, "I miss her."

Mark leaned back in his seat. He knew how close Alli and her sister were. "I may not have ever told you this, Alli, but I think you did a remarkable job raising her. I'm sure it wasn't easy."

"No," she agreed, "it wasn't. But if I had it to do all over again, I would. Kara was such a swell kid, but that didn't mean we didn't have our moments," she said grinning. "I thought I would never talk her out of getting her nose pierced." Alli didn't want to think of what could turn out to be her next crisis with Kara. Alli couldn't wait until she talked to Kara tomorrow to see how her date with the hottie had gone. "But I can't see Erika ever getting her nose pierced, do you?" she asked teasingly as she put thoughts of Kara from her mind.

Mark's eyes flashed with amusement as he glanced over at Erika, who was busy playing with a toy one of the waitresses had given her. "No, but I wonder what the fad is going to be when Erika reaches her teen years."

"Trust me, you don't want to know," Alli said chuckling.

Mark laughed. "You're probably right. We'll just have to wait and see."

Alli's heartbeat quickened. He had said it as though he expected her to be around during that time. Did he think she would still be working for him then? She didn't have time to ponder that question when a waitress walked up to take their order.

"Good afternoon, everyone."

Alli looked at the attractive waitress with the golden-blond hair and periwinkle-blue eyes who handed them plastic-coated menus. "Hello."

When the woman leaned over to fill their glasses

with water, Alli noticed that a pendant that had been tucked inside her dress slipped out. Alli thought the piece of jewelry, a heart that was etched with two intertwining roses, was simply beautiful. When the waitress walked off, Alli couldn't help wondering if the pendant had sentimental value like the one she was wearing, which had belonged to her mother.

"Gavin has a thing for her."

Mark's words jarred her attention. "For who?"

He smiled. "Our waitress. Her name is Valerie Raines and she arrived in town a few months ago. Gavin has a thing for her."

Alli lifted an arched eyebrow. "Sheriff Gavin O'Neal?"

Mark chuckled. "Yes. He makes sure he comes here every night for coffee. Before she arrived in town he didn't consume it as much as he does now." He chuckled again. "If he's not careful he might be headed for an addiction of another kind."

Alli nodded. She wondered if there was a particular woman out there that Mark had a *thing* for. She was well aware that he dated occasionally since she often screened the phone calls he received at the studio. He'd been known to date a number of gorgeous women and just last year his name had been linked to a senator's daughter. But all that had changed after he'd gotten Erika. His social life had practically become nonexistent.

"Do you have any idea what you want to order?"

She looked up from the menu. "I think I'll get a hamburger, a peach milkshake and for dessert, a slice of Manny's coconut-cream pie."

Mark set aside his menu. "I think I'm going to have the same."

* * *

"I think we wore her out," Mark said as he entered his home with a sleeping Erika in his arms.

"Hmm, it seems that way doesn't it? I think the circus did it."

As they were leaving the diner, Manny had called Mark over and given him tickets to the circus that was in Midland. Since Midland wasn't too far away, Mark thought it would be the perfect opportunity to put Alli's SUV on the road to break it in.

Instead of leaving his truck at the diner, he had left it in the Cattleman's Club parking lot. It was the first time Mark had been a passenger while Alli was a driver. On the way back, he had done the driving and had made a number of positive comments on how impressed he was with the way she had handled her new vehicle.

"Let me get her ready for bed," Alli said, taking Erika out of his arms. They touched in the process and the sexual tension that had been humming between them all evening increased.

"Do you need help with her?" Mark asked throatily, hoping Alli would say no. He needed to put distance between them to get his bearings. The conversation during the drive to and from Midland had been enjoyable, but he had been fully aware of the chemistry that stirred whenever they were together, and being in such close quarters hadn't helped. The spark he'd felt just now when she had taken Erika from him was almost too much.

"No, I can handle her all by myself," Alli said, cradling the sleeping baby in her arms. "Thanks for going with me to pick up my truck and thanks, too, for dinner and the circus. I had a wonderful time."

He nodded. "And I had a good time, too."

He wouldn't admit that he had spent most of his time watching her. As usual, she looked good and the skirt and blouse she was wearing emphasized her curves to perfection. The hem of the skirt was short enough to show off what he considered the best-looking legs he'd ever seen on a woman. He hated admitting it, but during the entire evening his mind had been filled with erotic fantasies of those legs wrapped around him while they made love. To his chagrin and dismay, he had been thinking about that a lot lately. Despite his effort, the fact that she was his employee was slowly fading to the background.

"Good night, Mark. I'll see you in the morning."

"Good night, Alli. I'll see you in the morning as well. "

As soon as she entered Erika's bedroom and closed the door, he quickly moved down the hallway, desperately needing the privacy and seclusion that he would find in his own bedroom.

Mark couldn't sleep. He had tried counting sheep, pigs, cattle and even little lambs, and nothing did the trick. It didn't help matters that earlier he had heard the sound of the shower in Alli's room again, and those visions that had played havoc on his mind two nights ago came storming back. At least the house was quiet, which meant she had settled down and one of them was getting some sleep.

But it seemed that sleep wasn't coming his way. He was sentenced to lie in bed wide awake and fight this overpowering physical attraction that he felt for her.

Physical attraction, hell! What he was beginning to feel was need, deep-in-the-gut need that a man felt for a woman he wanted. Alli was intensely woman, seductively female. No matter how much he tried, he couldn't ignore the way his body, his entire being, was craving another taste of her. It didn't take much to remember the feel of her mouth beneath his, soft, hot, delicious, and the texture of her skin, smooth and creamy, whenever he touched her. Then there had been the feel of her breasts, lush and firm, when they had pressed up against his chest. And last but not least, there was something about her smile. He was inherently drawn to it. The one she gave Erika was different than the one she gave him, which wasn't as easy and open, but nevertheless, it did things to him.

He changed positions and tried rearranging his pillows. Tomorrow was Sunday and with Alli in the house to take care of Erika, he would get to sleep late. But a part of him didn't want to sleep late. He wanted to get up and see Erika and Alli, have breakfast with them and spend time with them.

He didn't want to admit it but he had enjoyed their company today, and Alli's presence had been like a breath of fresh air. Unlike other women he'd dated, she didn't try to impress him. She had been able to make an impact by merely being herself.

Seeing that sleep was impossible, he got out of bed, slipped into his pajama bottoms and decided to go into the kitchen to get something to drink.

Alli couldn't sleep and decided to get up to check on Erika. She was easing out of the baby's room, closing the door behind herself, when she stopped, the cool wood floor beneath her bare feet suddenly feeling warm. She tensed, abruptly turned and her gaze collided with Mark's as he walked out of his bedroom.

For a long moment their gazes held, connected, interlocked with a fierce tension. Even from the few feet that separated them, she could smell his scent, and seeing him dressed in a pair of low-slung gray pajama bottoms wasn't helping matters. Not when his bare chest reminded her of when they had collided that morning he'd been about to shave.

And now, like then, her body tingled with full awareness of him as a man.

"I thought you were in bed asleep," Mark said, almost in a whisper.

She swallowed, trying to get both her brain and her mouth to function, and knew she needed to stop staring at his chest, especially the way a thin, hairy line made a path downward to disappear in the waistband of his pajamas. "I decided to check on Erika," she somehow managed to say.

Concern touched his features and he covered the distance to stand in front of her. "Why? Was something wrong? Is she okay?"

Erika is fine. I'm the one about to go up in flames, she wanted to say, meeting his gaze. "No, she's okay. I couldn't sleep and decided to check on her."

"Oh, I see."

Alli doubted that he did, but that was okay. Right now she needed to escape to her bedroom and fast. "Well, I'd better go back to bed. Good night."

"Good night, Alli." He stepped back to let her pass

but then, driven by a need he didn't understand, he reached out and touched her arm.

Mark felt it the moment their flesh connected, that spark. He heard the quick intake of her breath and knew she had felt it, too. And if that wasn't bad enough, the air around them seemed to change. It got thicker, overpowering, and pulsated with sexual energy of the most potent kind. He could breathe it, smell it, almost taste it.

The same way he desperately wanted to taste her.

Acting on something greater than instinct and driven by a need that suddenly took control of his entire body, he leaned down and captured her lips, urging and coaxing them to part under his, then tempting her tongue with his own. His fingers tangled in her hair as he held her immobile, determined to get his fill of what had been the cause of his sleepless nights.

His tongue took hers in firm strokes and when he heard a whimper from deep within her throat, he deepened the kiss, pulled her closer to the fit of him, flexed his hips and rocked hard against her, wanting her to know just what she was doing to him.

He refused to ease the pressure he was placing on her mouth and with each fragmented moan she released, he deepened the kiss more, fighting the thought that although this kiss was as good as it got, there was something else here, something he was feeling that went beyond sexual.

The sudden need to breathe overrode his urgency to continue tasting her and he slowly let go, but he didn't pull back, nor did he stop kissing her completely. His tongue made slow, teasing strokes to each corner of her mouth and he felt the deep shudder that passed through her.

"We broke the rules again, didn't we?" she said softly, releasing a shaky breath and burying her face in his chest.

He inhaled deeply as his arms tightened around her. She sounded so disappointed, so sad, and her entire body was trembling.

"I'm sorry, Mark. I allowed things to get out of hand again. I'll pack my things and leave in the morning."

Her words infiltrated his heat-infested mind and the beating of his heart almost stopped. Did she actually blame herself for this?

He sighed deeply and pulled her closer. No one was to blame, especially not her. Yes, they had broken the rules again, but at this point it didn't matter because he intended for them to keep breaking them. He didn't care about the strictly professional relationship they were supposed to have anymore. He knew that he might be making one of the biggest mistakes of his life, but he wanted her, this woman, in his arms, his bed. He wanted her to have an in-depth, intimate knowledge of him and he wanted an in-depth, intimate knowledge of her.

"Alli, look at me," he whispered softly.

It took a while but she finally lifted her head and met his gaze. "Now tell me, what do you see?"

Alli silently searched his face. What she saw was a very handsome man; a man with a big heart and a lot of love to share. But he was trying desperately to keep that love shut up inside. He was a man who could love with a passion if only he allowed himself to let go. He was also a man who cared but was determined to keep his emotions buried and unexposed. But what she saw more than anything was the man she had fallen in love with two years ago. A part of her wanted to expose those hidden emotions within him, bring them out in the open and destroy the heart-wrenching pain that engulfed his world. Then it hit her. She felt it and couldn't ignore it. Absurd as it might seem, for the moment, she believed it.

Mark needed her.

She inhaled deeply and finally responded by making him think about his own question. "You tell me what I *should* see, Mark."

Time stood still as he gazed at her, saying nothing, then after drawing in a ragged breath, he said, "You should see a man who doesn't give a damn about rules right now. A man who will have no regrets tomorrow. What you should see is a man who desperately wants you, who has wanted you for a long time and at this moment he can't breathe another breath unless he has you, in his arms, in his bed."

Knowing he had to be completely honest with her, he continued to speak. "I can't make you promises and I won't. I don't want, nor am I looking for, a serious, lasting relationship, which is the main reason I never wanted to become involved with you. But if you allow me, I'll introduce you to all the pleasures that a man and a woman can share. Pleasures you've denied yourself and pleasures I've denied myself as well. I haven't been with anyone for over a year, Alli, because every woman I dated I wanted to be you. I've wanted you that much."

Emotions clogged Alli's throat. In no way was he saying that he cared anything about her. In fact, he was letting her know that commitment of any kind was out of the question. But what he'd said touched her. He wanted her, and although there weren't promises of forever, she felt drawn to him nonetheless.

"I know that considering everything I've just said, I don't have any rights to ask anything of you, so I won't," he said, reclaiming her thoughts. "I'm going back to my room so you can think about what I'm offering. If you decide to accept my terms, then come to me. You don't have to knock, just open the door and walk on in."

He swallowed deeply and then said, "If you decide not to come, I'll understand. The decision is yours."

Before Alli could say anything, he had turned, reentered his bedroom and softly closed the door behind himself.

Alli breathed deeply. Mark was wrong. The decision wasn't hers. It belonged to her heart.

Eight

She wasn't coming.

Mark blinked, realizing that his gaze had been riveted on his bedroom door ever since he had left Alli standing in the hall. He glanced at the clock on the nightstand. Twenty minutes had passed.

His stomach tumbled in disappointment, but he accepted her decision. After all, he wasn't offering her anything except pleasure and for her that might not be enough.

But that was all he could give her.

He had made sure he thoroughly explained that, not wanting to take a chance on there being any misunderstandings. A misunderstanding would not be a good situation for either of them. He had wanted her to know the score.

Knowing sleep was impossible, he threw back the

covers and got out of bed to walk over to the window that overlooked the back of his property. From the moon's satiny glow, he could see the outlines of the meadows and valleys that were Hartman land. As a child he had loved it here, but as a teenager he had counted the days before he could leave. Both he and Matt had sworn never to return as long as their old man had lived. And they never had.

Mark's body jolted to attention when he heard his bedroom door opening and he held his breath, too afraid to turn around for fear he had just imagined the sound. But moments later when he heard the soft sound of bare footsteps touching the wood floor, and inhaled the scent that was distinctively Alli, he knew he wasn't imagining things.

With his pulse racing a mile a minute, he forced back the surge of desire that rammed his body as he slowly turned around. His gaze went to her face and watched as a nervous smile touched her lips.

"I'm here," she whispered softly, and the seductively quiet voice sent his pulse racing even more.

His breath hitched and the only words he could manage to say while his brain seemed not to be functioning were, "Thank you for coming."

His gaze then took in what she was wearing. She had changed from the tea-length nightgown and matching robe she'd had on earlier to a more seductive outfit. Now she was wearing a very short, red silk sleep shirt that did more than just complement her chocolate-brown skin. And with her five-eight height and long, gorgeous legs, the outfit looked both feminine and sexy on her.

"I didn't think you were coming," he said huskily, abruptly aware that the room was filled with the sound of their uneven breathing.

She smiled wryly and he saw the nervousness begin to ease from her features. "I wanted to put on something that I thought would be more appropriate."

Doesn't matter since I plan to remove every stitch from you, he thought, slowly dropping his gaze to rake it over her. Moments later he was staring back into the beautiful face that had haunted his dreams for nearly two years; whether he had wanted it to or not.

Is she sure about this? he wondered, as he swallowed the lump that suddenly appeared in his throat. He had to be certain. "Are you positive this is what you want?" he asked in a slightly hoarse voice.

"Yes, I'm positive." She lifted her chin and what he saw almost took his breath away. The same desire that he knew was lining his features was also lining hers. Tonight she had more to lose than he did, since he was fairly certain, could probably bet his ranch on it, that the woman standing before him was still a virgin. It all made sense. The way she always seemed unsure of herself when they kissed and how she would let him take the lead and eagerly followed. But then he had to admit, tonight would mean a lot to him as well. He had never introduced sexual pleasures to a virgin and hoped that he went above and beyond her expectations.

He decided to set the tone for what was about to follow. "If you're absolutely certain, come here."

With her gaze still holding his, she padded over to him. "Closer," he whispered as her soft feminine scent filtered into his nostrils. He watched her swallow, saw the thickness in her throat when she took another couple of steps, bringing her nearly face-to-face with him. But as far as he was concerned, that wasn't close enough.

"Closer," he whispered lower still.

She lifted an eyebrow, obviously confused. If she took another step, she would be all on top of him. A smile touched the corners of his mouth. That was the idea.

Mark watched as she drew a quivering breath and when she took another step, he automatically widened his stance and, as he'd known, she fit perfectly, positioning herself between his legs. He wanted her to feel the size of his erection and this way she couldn't miss it. And from the sudden look that appeared on her face, she hadn't.

The feel of Mark's erection pressed large, hard and throbbing against her middle sent a deep ache through Alli's body. It was an ache for something she couldn't name but wanted just the same. When she had eased between his open legs, her nightshirt had risen up past her thighs, beyond what was decent, and provided a provocative glimpse of her matching bikini panties. A surge of heat ripped through her and all she could think about was the degree of passion he was making her feel. To want him this much and be this close to having him were things she had only experienced in her dreams. Now she had to concede that reality was a whole lot better.

She had decided to do this, to become his lover for tonight, tomorrow, for however long he wanted. He might think of it as animal attraction, lust, an uncontrollable yearning or overwhelming desire, but for her she knew it was love. She loved this man with every ounce of her being and if this would be all they would ever share, then she was willing to make do. But just as he had given her a choice tonight, when it was time for her to leave she would give him the chance to make a choice as well. She believed that behind the stone wall surrounding his heart was the loving kindness of the man she knew he was.

"Feel it?"

His question jolted her to attention. She met his gaze. It was intense, hypnotic, arousing. She didn't doubt for an instant just what he was asking. "Yes, I feel it."

"Would you like to have it?"

She hesitated a second; not that she wasn't sure that she wanted it, but because she was surprised he would ask. She sucked in a deep breath when it seemed the throbbing tempo of the erection pressed against her increased and the size of it got larger. She tilted her head. "Yes, most definitely."

She watched as a smile touched his lips. "I hope you know what you're getting into because I plan to get all into you," he whispered huskily, before leaning down and kissing her with an urgency that almost made her swoon.

The way his tongue was taking her had desire—as potent as it could get—seeping into her pores, making her want things she never had before. And not knowing how it was possible, he pulled her closer to the fit of him as silk rubbed against silk, flesh against flesh, heat against heat. She felt it the instant he slid his hands up her thighs while deepening the kiss at the same time. She felt his fingers work their way beneath her shirt then inch toward the edge of her panties.

While changing clothes, she had been tempted to leave them off, which would have had her completely bare to his hands at this point. But it seemed nothing was going to stop him and he intended to have her bare anyway. And when his fingers eased past the waistband on her panties and he touched her intimately, she knew how it felt to place oneself in a man's hands.

She was wet, drenched, Mark thought as his fingers found their mark and gently eased inside of her. He shifted positions, widening his legs, as well as hers. He fought for control, clung to his last ounce of willpower when the moans she began making filled the room. The scent of her aroused body was permeating the air and it was like an aphrodisiac, stimulating every cell within him and amplifying his libido.

And then she did something he hadn't expected and wasn't prepared for. She shifted her body, reached out and wiggled her small hand into the opening of his silk pajama bottoms and grabbed hold of him. He could tell she was just as surprised by her actions as he was. But in no way did he intend to discourage her. Unlike her, he didn't have on a stitch of clothing beneath and all he could think about was the feel of her soft hand on his hard shaft. When she began running her fingers down the length of him, as if she needed to find out for herself what his erection was all about, he almost lost it.

With an animal groan that erupted deep from within his throat, he swept her into his arms. Never in his life had he ached so much for a woman and, clinging to his last shred of self-control, he carried her over to his bed.

Alli buried her face into Mark's hair-covered chest, now fully understanding how if felt to be swept off her feet. From the moment she had walked into his room, he had made her feel like the most desired woman in the world. Now being engulfed in his strong arms, she felt doubly so.

When he placed her on the bed and joined her there, she knew her endurance was about to be tested. He reached out and began unbuttoning her shirt and then removed it from her body, leaving her clad only in her panties. She wondered if he realized that he was staggering her senses.

He raised high above her, after letting his gaze roam over her near-naked body, his hazel eyes locked on her face. "If I do or suggest doing anything you aren't comfortable with, promise that you'll let me know," he whispered huskily as he brushed her hair aside and moved his lips closer to her ear.

"I promise."

Her body began shuddering when the palm of his hand moved slowly down her bare arms at the same time his warm breath trailed over her neck. "And I want you to promise if I tell you *not* to stop that you won't," she whispered, feeling herself lose what little control she'd been holding on to.

She felt the imprint of his smile against her neck. "You sure about that?"

"Positive."

"I don't think you know what you'll be asking for," he said, swathing her neck with a series of wet butterfly kisses.

"Yes, I do," she whispered when his mouth started moving lower. "I'll be asking for more of you."

He lifted his head, met her eyes and penetrated them

with a deep intensity. "I promise," he whispered. And then, as if in slow motion, he connected his mouth to hers.

In Alli's mind this kiss was different. Using the tip of his tongue, he invaded, teased and explored every corner, nook and crevice of her mouth, especially those areas she hadn't been aware were insanely sensitive until now. And with every movement of his tongue, he elicited her reaction; he seemed to feed on it and, in no time at all, he had her moaning out sounds she wasn't aware she was capable of making.

The multitude of what she was feeling stunned her, captivated her and filled her with a need that was all consuming.

As slowly as he had entered her mouth, he was pulling out, but didn't go far. He trailed kisses down her neck, easing down her chest and, when his lips came to her breasts, he pulled her close and took one into this mouth, licking, sucking and nibbling, one then the other.

No man had ever touched her there, let alone kissed her, and the feel of Mark's mouth on her nipples—as well as what he was doing to them—had her sucking in deep breaths. Winding her arms around his neck, he intensified his mouth tugging on her, making her feel erotic sensations all the way to her toes. He had a very talented mouth, she quickly concluded, and when he finally pulled back, she suddenly felt a deep sense of loss.

"You taste good," he whispered, the intensity in her eyes making her even hotter. "And I want to get inside of you, Alli."

The heat of his words, uttered so close to her ear, made her skin vibrate and her stomach quicken in anticipation. "And I want you, Mark," she whispered back, still swooning from the drugging sensations of his kisses to her mouth and breasts.

"I want to make sure you're completely ready for me, baby."

She met his gaze, wondering why he would do that when her body was already overheated. "Remember, your promise," he whispered softly as he leaned down and his lips began skimming softly, gently, heated over her bare flesh. He stopped when he reached her navel and plied it with wet kisses that brought her to complete awareness.

While Mark had her full attention, Alli was aware that he was removing her panties, and he pulled back slightly to ease them down her legs. Then he stood and she watched as he eased his pajama bottoms from his body, and they became a puddle at the foot of the bed. The lamp in the room gave her enough light to see him and she began breathing hard. Never had she thought that a male's body could be so beautiful, so well defined and so masculine. She had thought he was built before, but now, seeing him completely naked sent a delicious shiver all the way through her.

She wanted to reach out and touch him, run her hands down the expanse of his hairy chest, along the muscles of his shoulders, and as her gaze moved lower to that part of him that she had brazenly touched earlier, she inhaled deeply at the size, wondering how on earth...

She blinked when he moved and reached over to the nightstand, opened the drawer and pulled out a condom packet. Anticipation ran rampant through her as he put it on.

Then he lifted his head and their eyes met. The way

he looked at her made erotic sensations engulf her. He joined her on the bed again. Leaning back on his haunches, he continued to look at her. Instead of making her nervous and embarrassed about not having on a stitch of clothing, she was eagerly anticipating his next move.

He made it.

He leaned down and slipped his hand between her thighs, touching her intimately. She sucked in a deep breath when he gently inserted a finger inside of her, and instinctively her hips moved, her thighs opened to accommodate him.

If she thought he had a talented mouth, then his fingers were a close second. She began feeling dazed at the way he was making her feel with each movement. The feelings it was evoking within her were beyond belief and, when he drove a little deeper and touched an area inside of her that had to be some type of pleasure point to make her body feel this way, she felt a gush of blood rush through all parts of her, centering right where his finger was located. The intensity of it caused her moan almost to become a sob. Never had she been so unreservedly aroused before.

"I think you're ready for me now."

She met the intensity of his gaze, thinking that she'd been ready...for nearly two years. Long ago she had made up her mind to have him if he ever made the move. She was tired of living a lonely unexciting life. She wanted to share this most intimate and personal act with the man she loved. And although he might not love her, tonight he was making her feel wanted, desired and beautiful.

Before she could think another thing, he eased over

her, positioning himself between her open thighs, supporting his weight on his elbows. The heady thought of what they were about to do sent shivers racing through her. He must have felt them and looked down to meet her gaze.

She closed her eyes, but he whispered, "Open them. I want to be looking at you the entire time. I want to see your reaction, your response to my loving you this way, Alli."

She opened her eyes and wound her arms around his neck. Then she felt it, his attempt to ease inside of her, but struggling to do so because her body was too tight. He eased out a little and then tried again, the huge tip of him hot and eager at her entrance.

Alli watched perspiration forming on his forehead, his gaze still holding hers. "We're going to try this again. Hold on, baby."

She did.

And she breathed deeply as she felt him entering her once more, this time not letting the barrier get in his way. Inch by sensual inch, he continued going deeper, breaking through, overwhelming her with his size as well as his possession. She felt the pain and tried not to show it on her face but knew she did anyway. And when a tear she couldn't control eased from the corner of her eye, he paused.

Apprehension about what she knew he was thinking about doing ruled her mind. Still holding his gaze she whispered, "Don't stop." And when he still hesitated, she added, "Remember your promise."

She watched as he breathed in deeply, and then he

was slowly penetrating her again, moving deeper, painfully so, until he was completely sheathed inside of her.

"Are you okay?"

Looking into his eyes, she nodded, seeing the concern and the caring there. She noticed the pain was going away and what she was beginning to feel was a deep driving need right in the place where their bodies were joined. He must have felt it, too, because she felt him move, slowly at first, gentle, long, even strokes that started a heated flame escalating through her, as if feeding on what she needed. Feeding on it as well as intensifying it.

Her body began writhing at the sensations she was feeling and all she could think of was having more of him, him going deeper inside of her, touching every part of her that existed. He increased the tempo, the intensity of it took her breath away. He stroked deeper, thrusting back and forth. She cried out at the tension she felt building inside of her and the only thing she could think about was how much she loved him and how he was making her feel. Mark had captured her heart and was initiating her into the throes of womanhood in its truest form.

Then something happened. Something snapped inside of her and her first instinct was to scream but she knew doing so would wake the baby. Instead she groaned and moaned out loud as sensations racked through her and she muttered his name from deep within her throat.

"Mark!"

"That's it, baby, let go. I'm here with you all the way."

And he was.

He grabbed her hips as he continued to thrust inside of her, over and over again, completely filling her with him and taking everything she was offering. He shuddered one, twice, a third time then called her name, the sound a deep wrenching moan from his lips. She felt his body jerk, the same way hers was, and knew that what they were experiencing was an orgasm of the highest magnitude, the most explosive kind.

Their moans of pleasure filled the room and when he lowered his mouth to hers, the joy of what they were sharing brought more tears to her eyes. She knew that she would love Mark Hartman forever, no matter what.

Some time during the night, Mark woke up and glanced down at the woman snuggled against him. After making love to her that first time, he had picked her up and carried her into the bathroom where he'd run bathwater for both of them. In his huge whirlpool tub, he'd washed the soreness from her body, glorying in them sharing such an intimate act as bathing together.

Then he had wrapped her in a huge towel and taken her back to his room to dry her and had slipped her nightshirt on her. Evidently assuming she was being dismissed, he had reached out to capture her wrist when she had headed for the door. After kissing her deeply, to show her how wrong that assumption was, he had picked her up in his arms and taken her to bed with him, cuddling her gently beside him until they had gone to sleep. He could even admit that he had gotten the best sleep he'd had in years.

He would never forget the expression on Alli's face when she had experienced her first orgasm. That sight would remain in his brain forever. She had come apart in his arms the same way she did everything else, with breathtaking enthusiasm.

They had broken the rule of maintaining a strictly professional relationship, but that didn't bother him. In fact, he was waiting for her to wake up so they could break the rules again. He smiled, not ever remembering wanting a woman so much.

He closed his eyes and pinched the bridge of his nose, refusing to think where all this could lead…and where it couldn't lead. How would they go back to spending hours in the office together without him needing to touch her, spread her out on his desk and enjoy a little afternoon delight? How in the hell was he going to control his deep craving for her? It was different when he just had his fantasies, but now he had sampled what he considered the most delicious morsel he'd ever had the pleasure of tasting.

And that included Patrice.

Patrice had never really enjoyed making love and only did so because she felt it was her duty. But Alli was totally different. She had to be the most passionate woman he knew and he could tell she thoroughly enjoyed making love with him. He was going to enjoy tapping into her passion.

A sudden thought unnerved him. What if now that he had unleashed her sensual side, she decided that making love with him wasn't enough? What if she decided that since he wouldn't commit to her, dating other men was the thing to do? His jaw tightened at the thought of her in bed with another man, another man holding her in his arms this way, another man making her scream out his name.

Mark inhaled in a deep breath. He would have to make sure that while Alli lived under his roof and worked at the studio, he was the only man she needed. The only man she wanted.

Satisfied with that decision, he shifted positions, reached out and held her in his arms as he drifted off to sleep.

Alli slowly opened her eyes and glanced up. Mark was lying beside her and had been resting on his elbows looking at her, evidently watching her sleep…or waiting for her to wake up.

"Good morning, Alli."

The sound of his voice, deep, rich and ultra sexy, sent shivers through her. She tilted her head and glanced at the clock on his nightstand. She guessed that technically it was morning although it was just five o'clock. "Good morning," she said, trying to rid her voice of that drowsy sound.

"I've been waiting for you to wake up," he said, leaning down, close to her lips.

"You have?" Her pulse began racing, especially when he shifted positions slightly and placed his leg over hers. The contact of flesh on flesh sent more shivers escalating through her.

"Yes. I want to make love to you again."

She swallowed. "You do?"

He chuckled. "Oh yes, I do." And then he was kissing her and she forgot everything except how he was making her feel.

The only thing she remembered after that was him pulling back long enough to remove her nightshirt and his pajama bottoms and put on a condom, then him using his hands to drive her to what had to be the highest sexual peak. It was at that moment that he eased his body over hers and slowly entered her, not finding the impediment he had the night before.

As he continued to kiss her and thrust back and forth inside her body, his tongue did likewise, moving back and forth between her parted lips. She felt emotions in every part of her as he deliberately drove her over the edge. When she lost control and exploded in what seemed like a thousand pieces, she cried out his name. With a deep animal groan, he followed her and she felt the tremors that slammed into him ram into her as well.

And when he pulled her closer as he continued to pump into her as they groaned out their pleasures, she had a feeling that Mark Hartman wasn't through with her yet.

And wouldn't be for a long time.

Nine

Mark walked into Erika's bedroom and saw Alli and Erika sitting on the floor going through his niece's toy box.

The sheer beauty of everything they had shared left him breathless when he thought about it. After making love to her again that morning, once, twice, he had been driven to make love to her over and over again until they had both succumbed to total exhaustion. And when they heard the sound of Erika's voice coming over the monitor, exclaiming she wanted to eat, he had encouraged Alli to sleep a little longer while he took care of his niece. It was halfway through breakfast when Alli had walked into the kitchen, looking utterly gorgeous and apologizing for having overslept. He had taken great pleasure in pulling her into his arms and kissing the apology right off her lips.

"Da-da!"

Automatically, as if it were the most natural thing in the world to do, he crossed the room to them and crouched down to place a kiss on Alli's lips.

"Kiss me, Da-da," Erika said, wrapping her arms around his neck so he could pick her up. Her request caught him up short. He had never gone far in showing that sort of affection to his niece. "Kiss me, Da-da," she said again. A little more adamant this time.

Not wanting to disappoint her, he placed a kiss on her cheek and she let out a shriek of happiness. He quickly handed her to Alli. "I just wanted to let you know I need to go to the studio for a second. I'll be back in an hour."

Alli nodded. "How is the temporary help working out?"

He shrugged, deciding not to mention the mix up in appointments the woman had made on Friday. "She'll do until you get back. I'm hoping to hear something from Mrs. Tucker in a couple of weeks whether or not she'll be returning to Royal."

"Do you think that she will?"

"I'm hoping that she does. That would be the best thing that could happen."

To Alli, the best thing that could happen was for Mark to fall in love with her and want to keep her around, but she knew that was really reaching for the stars. "What do you think about grilling something for dinner?"

Mark raised his eyebrow. "We usually eat whatever Mrs. Sanders prepares on Friday."

Alli smiled. "I thought it would be nice if you grilled hamburgers or hot dogs. Something simple. I'd be glad to prepare all the trimmings."

"Trimmings like what?"

"Potato salad, corn on the cob, bake beans."

Mark smiled. "Sounds delicious."

Alli returned his smile. "Then it's settled. I'll have everything set up when you get back."

"Okay." Then he leaned over and kissed her before turning and walking out the door.

"So how was your date last night, Kara?"

"Do you really want to know, Alli, or are you calling to lecture me again like I've never gone out on a date before? I know more about dating than you do."

Alli opened her mouth to say something then changed her mind and closed it. In a way Kara was right. How could someone who'd never dated give anyone advice about it? And spending a night in Mark's arms didn't really count.

"I'm sorry, Alli. That was tacky of me to say such a thing. Tacky and thoughtless especially when you sacrificed your social life for me."

Hearing Kara's apology she said, "Hey, it's okay and you're right, I'm no expert. So how was the date?"

She spent the next few minutes listening to Kara tell her how the hottie named Cameron took her to a fraternity party on campus and what a perfect gentleman he'd been. Kara also mentioned that they had another date this weekend and would be going to the movies.

"Look, this might not be the best time to remind you, but you were coming home this weekend," Alli decided to say.

"Oh my gosh, I forgot all about that." Moments later she asked. "Do I really need to come home?"

Alli sighed deeply. This would be Kara's first visit

back since school had started and Alli wanted to see her. Besides, she hoped to have a surprise for her. The extra money she was making as Erika's nanny meant that she could swing the payments for a used car for Kara and had wanted to surprise her with it . "No, not if you don't want to."

"It's not that I don't want to come home, Alli, but I forgot and told Cameron I'd go to the movies with him this weekend. Please don't get upset with me about it."

Alli considered Kara's words. She knew that she and her sister loved each other but even the strongest loving relationships could suffer from the strain of opposing opinions about things. "I'm not upset and I understand you wanting to stay there and go out with your new friend."

"Thanks for understanding, Alli. You're the greatest and I love you."

Alli smiled, not really understanding. "And I love you, too, kiddo."

After hanging up the phone, Alli walked over to the window and looked out. Was she being unfair to Kara by expecting more of her than she should? It was natural for girls to be interested in boys and vice versa. Although Kara had dated while in high school, she'd never let anything, especially boys, interfere with her studies.

Alli turned when she heard the gentle knock on her bedroom door. "Come in."

Mark entered the room looking as gorgeous as usual. "I finally got Erika off to sleep. She was determined to play all night." He grinned. "If I didn't know better, I'd think that applesauce you gave her was laced with some sort of energy booster. She's been a live wire all afternoon.

Alli couldn't help but agree. When Mark had returned from the studio, she'd been busy in the kitchen preparing the trimmings. It hadn't taken him any time to put the hot dogs and hamburgers on the grill. He'd even cooked a couple of steaks. Afterward, they had sat outside on the patio. For a handful of seconds while sitting across from him, it had run through her mind just how much of a real family they seemed to be. When he'd mentioned something about Gavin calling a Cattleman's Club meeting for tomorrow night, she had been reminded of just how outside of his world she really was.

She watched as he stepped farther into the room. "I was wondering if you wanted to eat a slice of apple pie with me," he said. "And I know I've already told you, but I have to tell you again how good the pie was."

She smiled at the compliment. "Thanks. And thanks for inviting me to have another slice of pie but I don't think I can eat anything else." She tilted her head and looked at him. "I'm wondering how you can."

He chuckled. "Well, it was just that good. You knew apple pie is my favorite, didn't you?"

"Yes."

He leaned against her bedpost. "And how did you know that?"

She chuckled. "Mark, I'm your assistant. I'm supposed to know these things. Besides, I asked you once when Mrs. Gallant wanted to bake you that pie for giving those self-defense classes to the ladies at that senior-citizens center the first of the year. Don't you remember me asking you about it?"

He shook his head. "No." Evidently, that had to be one of those times when he'd been concentrating on her and not on what she'd been saying, he thought.

"Will you be available Tuesday for Erika's doctor's appointment?"

Her question jarred his attention to her. He raised his eyebrow. "Erika has a doctor's appointment?"

"Yes, the doctor's office called last week as a reminder. It's for her routine checkup." Alli smiled. "She'll be celebrating her first birthday next month."

Mark sighed. Had it been nearly three months already? Erika had been a bouncing eight-month-old baby when he had flown to California to get her. "I've never gone to her doctor appointments. Mrs. Tucker always took her and afterwards told me what the doctor said. I prefer doing things that way."

Alli nodded. She knew it was another technique he was using to keep a semblance of distance between him and his niece. "I would think you'd want to meet her pediatrician and hear what he has to say about Erika's health."

Mark frowned. "Why? You think there might be something wrong with her?"

Alli heard the panic in his voice. She wondered if he was hearing it. "No. Like I said it's a routine checkup. She'll probably get a vaccination of some sort."

Mark nodded. "Then there's no reason for me to be there. I'm sure you can handle things."

She opened her mouth to push the issue, then decided not to push now. She would push later. If nothing else, she was determined to make him see just how deeply he cared for his niece.

Mark continued to gaze at Alli, getting turned on by the minute just looking at her. She was wearing the tank top and cutoff jeans she'd had on earlier, which meant she hadn't taken her bath yet.

Deciding that he was a man of action, he walked across the room to stand in front of her. "If I can't interest you in eating a slice of pie with me, can I interest you in something else?"

He could tell that her curiosity was piqued when she lifted an arched eyebrow. "Something else like what?"

"A bath."

She chuckled as she slumped back against the windowsill. "Are you suggesting that I need one?"

"No," he said, taking a closer step to her. "I was suggesting that you take a bath. With me."

A smile curved her lips. "And just what will I get out of such a venture?"

He shook his head, chuckling, remembering. "Do you have to ask after last night and this morning?"

Mark saw an intense look appear on her face and he knew she was reliving the memories just as he was. "So, are you game?"

Alli knew she was more than game. She was becoming putty in his hands and she didn't have any regrets. "You're going to have to convince me it's something that I should do," she said, knowing she was giving him a challenge—a challenge he wouldn't hesitate in meeting.

"Convincing you is no problem, Alli," he whispered softly, reaching out, taking hold of her wrist and pulling her closer to him. His hands slid under her tank top, finding her bare, just as he thought. He hadn't been able to take his eyes off her chest while eating, seeing how the tips of her nipples were pressing against her top. He'd known that she was braless.

He watched her eyes as he caressed those same nipples, rubbing his fingers over the protruding tips, feeling them harden. "Remember how my mouth was on them last night, Alli, and how my tongue teased and tasted them?" He continued to let his hand fondle her, making her feel what he was feeling, getting her as aroused as he was. "Do you remember?"

"Yes, I remember," she answered in a raspy voice.

He liked the sound of it. "And do you remember how I kissed you and the number of times I kissed you?"

"Yes."

"Good, because I want to kiss you now. Part your lips for me, Alli, and let me in."

The moment she parted her lips, he leaned closer and his tongue slid heatedly over hers and the moment she released a deep moan, he went inside her mouth, kissing her with a hunger that she felt all the way to her toes. Pulling her closer to him, she couldn't help but cradle her thighs against the hardness of his aroused body.

She shuddered when sensations seeped through her pores, blood gushed through her veins and her pulse escalated to a point that had her sighing in pleasure. He kept kissing her until she was almost weak in the knees. It was only then that he pulled back.

He dropped his hands to his side. "Now will you take that bath with me?"

They stared at each other. Alli knew what her response would be, but she decided to show him rather than tell him. She leaned closer, framed his face with her hands, then kissed him with the same intensity that he had kissed her earlier.

Suddenly he broke off the kiss and he led her by the hand out of her bedroom into his. The first thing she noticed was the wood blazing in the fireplace. It had been warm earlier that day but the night had brought in cooler air.

He didn't stop until they reached his bathroom. She watched as he began running the bathwater in the tub that could fit two people easily. He turned to her, and without saying a word, began removing her clothes. When she was completely naked, she eased up to him to get some of his heated warmth. He gently lifted her and placed her in the tub.

She watched him remove his own clothing as his gaze locked on her with restrained hunger. She eased into the bubbles, thinking they might offer relief for her overheated body. She raised an eyebrow when he placed several condom packets on the edge of the tub.

"Lesson number two," he said, as his smile widened. "We have the freedom of making love at any time and any place on this ranch as long as we're protected from prying eyes." He joined her in the tub, grabbing the scented soap and lathering up his hands.

When he pulled her to face him, curving her legs around his waist and began rubbing the bubbles all over her, she let out a sigh. "We do?" Her breathing escalated at the way he was rubbing his soapy hands over her stomach, arms and breasts.

"Yes, we do," he whispered. His gaze held hers so she could see the intense desire in his eyes. "Now let me prove it."

And it didn't take long for him to do so.

Sheriff Gavin O'Neal glanced around the table, meeting the gazes of all the men present. Their Texas Cattleman's Club meeting was scheduled for Wednesday, but he thought he should share the lab's report with everyone as soon as possible.

"As all of you know, Mark found a syringe on the Windcrofts' ranch. The lab report came in today and their findings indicate it contains traces of potassium chloride, the same drug used to kill Jonathan."

It was Jake who spoke. "That makes Nita Windcroft a prime suspect."

Gavin nodded. "Yes, but I'm also looking at the possibility that someone might be framing her."

Logan leaned in. "Who?"

"Whoever is responsible for killing Jonathan. What could be better than to plant evidence on a major suspect? And if that's the case, then the person who put it there expects us to fall for it."

"And when we don't?" Connor Thorne asked.

Gavin met his gaze. "Then there's the likelihood they'll try again to make it seem like Nita did it."

Mark sat back in his chair. "Shouldn't we tell Nita so she'll know what to expect?"

Gavin shook his head. "No, because for now there's still a chance she might be guilty and want us to think she's being framed."

Mark sighed deeply. "Just so you'll know, last night Alli asked me about the rumors that are going around that Nita might be responsible for Jonathan's death. Alli went with me out to the Windcroft ranch and got to talk to Nita. According to Alli, Nita has heard the rumors and maintains she is innocent. Alli knows her better than I do and she believes her. She says there is no way Nita could have done it."

Gavin nodded again. "Then it is up to us to catch the

right person and prove Nita Windcroft's innocence. This is a listing of all Nita's clients," he said, passing copies of the list around the table. As you can see she has plenty of them. I want all of you to take a look at it and at our next meeting we'll discuss anyone who we might want to add to the suspect list."

"Hey, Jake, I see your opponent's name on the list. Can you believe Gretchen Halifax owns a horse that she keeps boarded at the Windcrofts' farm?" Connor said, chuckling. "I thought the lady-who-wants-to-be-mayor was too dignified to mount a horse."

"Yeah," Logan said, joining in. "And can you believe her horse is named Silver Dollar?"

Mark shook his head, smiling. "Figures."

Gavin shifted in his chair, deciding to bring the meeting back to order. "There's another reason I called this meeting tonight. The map has been returned."

"What?" The exclamation was uttered by five men.

"Yes, I got a call from Aaron Hill, the director of the Royal Museum. Hill says the map mysteriously returned today with a note."

"What note?" Thomas Devlin asked.

"A handwritten note of apology."

"Did the person say why they stole it in the first place?" Jake asked, shaking his head.

"Yes, the reason given was to keep it out of the hands of the real thieves," Gavin replied, placing the note in the middle of the table.

Logan chuckled. "At least we know for certain the person who stole it was really a woman. Only a female would see the logic in that."

The other five men at the table nodded in agreement.

"I had the handwriting on this note compared to those threatening notes that have been sent to Nita Windcroft. According to the lab, this note was definitely written by a woman and the notes Nita received were written by a man."

"Is there anything you need for us to do, Gavin?" Mark asked, checking his watch. He was looking forward to spending time with Alli again. He was still having memories of the bath they had shared last night and the lovemaking that had followed.

"No, that's about it other than to keep both your eyes and ears open and report anything. I won't rest until the person responsible for Jonathan's death is brought to justice."

"And just so you guys will know," Connor said, looking around the table. "I'm leaving to go out of town for a while. I have business to take care of in Virginia, but I hope to be back in a few weeks."

Gavin rose. "Well, that ends tonight's meeting." No sooner had he said those words, Mark was out of his chair headed for the door.

"You're in a hurry tonight, aren't you, Mark?" Jake called out.

"Yes, I guess you can say that," Mark replied over his shoulder without stopping or looking back.

Mark swung around and faced Alli, his eyes locked on hers. "What do you mean you can't take Erika to her doctor's appointment this morning?"

He tried not to notice how much of her thigh he saw when she crawled out of his bed and how her hair was tumbled around her face. When he had gotten in from the meeting last night, Erika had been asleep and Alli had been awake waiting for him…in his bed. And this was the first opportunity she'd had to get out of it.

"I know this is last minute and I do apologize, but I got a call from the bank yesterday reminding me that I needed to be there first thing this morning to sign those loan papers."

He lifted an eyebrow as she passed him on her way to the bathroom. He hurried after her. "What loan papers?"

She stared at him before walking into the bathroom where she intended to have a few private moments. "I'm getting Kara a used car. She could use one to get around on campus. Nothing fancy and definitely something I can afford since the payments on my new one will be low thanks to your friendship with that car dealer."

"I would have loaned you the money for that," he said as if he were in the habit of making car loans.

"Yes, well, I thought it best if I went to a financial institution, Mark, considering everything."

"Everything like what?"

"Our relationship. When Mrs. Tucker returns or when you find a permanent babysitter things between us will go back as they used to be. Besides, all I'm asking is for you to take Erika over to the doctor's office. Once I sign those papers I will join you there and take over. Now if you'll excuse me, I need to use the bathroom." She closed the bathroom door behind herself.

Mark's jaw tightened and his hands balled into fists at his side. He knew he was handling this badly, but he couldn't help it. First of all, he didn't want Alli reminding him that their relationship would be changing in a month or so. Secondly, he didn't want to take Erika to the doctor's office. He didn't want to sit in the waiting room with all those other people who would be parents and have them assume Erika was his daughter when he didn't know the first thing about being a dad. What if they tried making small talk about stuff he was supposed to know?

Damn, he wasn't looking forward to this particular assignment.

Mark sat in the doctor's office holding Erika in his lap. There were only a few people there and so far no one had been talkative. One woman had commented on how cute Erika looked. He had glanced down and noticed her pink coveralls, pink socks, white sneakers and the pink bows in her hair and had smiled proudly. She did look cute.

He glanced at his watch. Alli had said that she would be arriving around ten and it was almost that time. He hoped she got there before Erika's name was called.

"Erika Hartman."

"No such luck," Mark muttered quietly, glancing at the door beside the reception station and seeing a nurse standing there holding a patient's chart. "Looks like we're up, kid," he whispered softly, standing and holding Erika tightly as he maneuvered the diaper bag onto his shoulder.

"We're here," he decided to call out so the nurse wouldn't think they had disappeared.

The woman smiled when she saw Erika. "Well, hello little Miss Hartman. How have you been?" She then offered Mark her hand. "Hi, I'm Laurie, Dr. Covert's nurse. I don't think we've met."

And we wouldn't be meeting now if I'd had my way, Mark thought, accepting the woman's handshake. "No, we haven't. I won't be here with her long today. Her nanny is on the way."

Laurie nodded as she took Erika from Mark. "All right, but we can go ahead and get started. Follow me to an examination room."

Moments later, Mark stood on the sideline as Laurie undressed Erika. "She's such a happy baby," the nurse commented. "I remember the first time Mrs. Tucker brought her in here. The poor thing was crying so much we had to calm her down before we could check her and that was only a few months ago. You've done well in helping her to adjust."

"Thank you."

Mark turned around when the examination-room door opened, hoping it was Alli, but instead an older man he knew to be the doctor walked in. "Good morning, I'm Dr. Covert, and I understand it's time for this little lady's physical."

Mark continued to stand to the side and watched Erika get placed on a scale to be weighed, get her lungs checked and her head measured. "She seems to be developing nicely," the doctor said smiling.

The only bad moment was when the nurse had to give Erika a measles vaccination. She let out a loud wail but her tears quickly dried up when Laurie gave her a rubber ball to play with.

"Hmm, let's see," Dr. Covert was saying. "She's eleven months old so she should be standing alone—or at least trying to—responding to simple instructions, taking a few steps and saying mama and dada to the correct parent."

"She's not doing that," Mark decided to say.

The doctor lifted his gaze from Erika's chart and met Mark's eyes. "She's not doing what?"

"Saying those things correctly."

"She's not?"

"No."

The older man lifted a bushy eyebrow. "She's calling you mama and your wife dada?"

"No, I don't have a wife, just a nanny. And Erika's calling me dada but I'm not her daddy, I'm her uncle."

The doctor smiled. "That's natural. She sees you as a father figure, the one person who is constant in her life. Whenever she calls you dada just tell her your name, or the name you want her to call you."

"I've been doing that," Mark said, glancing at his watch again.

"Then just continue. She'll eventually catch on. Within the next month she'll start forming other sounds and I'm sure she'll start calling you by your name or at least she'll make attempts to do so. Just be patient with her."

Mark nodded. "What else will she try to do?"

"She'll try responding to simple instructions."

Mark chuckled. "Hey, she's doing that now."

"Then you have a very smart girl on your hands."

Mark beamed proudly. "Yes, she sure is that. What about walking? She's standing alone and has even tried taking a couple of steps while holding on to something. Is there anything I can do to motivate the process?"

Dr. Covert chuckled. "Try not carrying her wherever she wants to go, that will usually work."

Mark nodded. "All right. Is there anything else?"

"No, that's it. Your niece seems to be in good health

and after her visit next month we'll only need to see her every six months."

"What about foods? Is there anything she shouldn't have?"

The doctor spent the next few minutes explaining what foods were the best for Erika to eat and how they aided in her body's development, as well as those foods Mark should avoid giving her.

The examination-room door suddenly opened and Alli breezed in. "Sorry I'm late."

Mark waved away her apology and smiled. "That's fine. Things weren't so bad and Dr. Covert and I were having a little chat."

"Did you know we shouldn't give Erika honey until after her first birthday, and that honey can contain spores that cause botulism poisoning in babies?" Mark switched positions in bed to ask Alli.

Alli couldn't help but smile. It didn't take a Ph.D. to figure out that taking his niece to the doctor had certainly been an adventure for Mark. He hadn't stopped talking about it…at least he hadn't brought it up during the time they had made love. Now she didn't feel so bad about manipulating her time at the bank so he'd be the one to take Erika to the doctor once she'd discovered his calendar had been clear that morning.

"Yes, I knew it," Alli replied. "However, such a situation happening is rare."

Mark's expression turned serious. "Yeah, but it can happen. I'm going to have to remember that."

Alli shook her head smiling. She hoped he wasn't thinking of getting rid of all the honey in the house.

"Erika is almost a year old now. She'll be able to have honey pretty soon."

"Hmm, I don't know," Mark said. "Just because she'll be a little older how do we know for certain she won't get that botulism stuff?"

"We won't. We just have to believe that the doctor knows what he's talking about."

"Yeah, I guess you're right." He reached out and pulled Alli into his arms, tight against his body. "I'm tired of talking. I want to do something else," he said, leaning over and placing small kisses along her ear and neck.

"Again?"

Mark pulled back slightly, his expression turning serious again. "Do you think I want to make love to you too often?"

Alli smiled. "No, I was just kidding." When he didn't move but continued to stare at her as if he hadn't believed her, she said, "Honest, Mark, I was just kidding. I want you as much as you want me and every time you want to make love I'm right there with you. Why would you think you want to do it too often?"

He sighed deeply and met her gaze. "Patrice always said I did. She didn't like making love with me."

His words stunned Alli. She couldn't imagine any woman not wanting to make love with Mark, especially the woman who'd been his wife. "But why?"

He shrugged. "She didn't like sex."

Alli reached out and wrapped her arms around his neck. "Well, I happen to like it, but only with you." She could tell her words pleased him.

"No kidding?"

"No kidding. Can I prove it?"

She could tell her question caught him by surprise. "Well, uh, yes, I suppose so."

"Good, then lay back and enjoy. Keep in mind that I still lack a lot of expertise in this, but I'm finding that I have an excellent teacher."

Mark didn't get a chance to say anything. Her mouth captured his as she got on top of him. Incredible, he thought, loving her taste and thinking that he would never get tired of kissing her, but evidently she had other ideas and slowly pulled her mouth from his.

And then she was kissing the area around his ear, taking her tongue and licking it while whispering just what she wanted to do to him, what she planned to do to him. Her words and the feverish pitch of her voice inflamed him and he felt himself getting harder. She must have felt it, too, and adjusted her thighs to cradle his, while at the same time thrusting her hips against him so he could feel the contact of flesh touching flesh.

"I remember the first time I got on a horse," she whispered. "Do you remember your first time?"

He was trying to maintain his control but the feel of the tip of her tongue sliding alongside his ear was driving him crazy, and the way her naked body was fitting intimately to his wasn't helping matters. "Yes, I remember."

"Do you also remember how it felt to have such a huge animal beneath you?"

When her soft hand slid down his body and she took hold of his aroused staff, he gasped, then said huskily. "Yes."

"I do, too, and being on top of you this way reminds me what it felt like and it makes me want to do something."

She was rubbing her fingers up and down him, as if

she needed to know the shape, the texture and the degree of his heat. Her curiosity was pushing him over the edge. "Do something like what?"

"Ride you."

She reached over and took a condom pack off the nightstand and within minutes she had slipped it on him, almost driving him crazy in the process. "Now where were we?" she asked, shifting her body until she was over him again, locking his hips between her thighs. She braced herself above him and opened her legs wider.

Holding his gaze, she slowly eased her body down, taking him inside of her while listening to his labored breathing. Impatient, he thrust his hips upward, trying to hurry the connection, and since she was wet and slick, he drove easily into her to the hilt.

"I don't think you can go any farther," she panted, still looking at him. Their bodies were connected tight. But that didn't stop her from clenching her muscles around him, making him groan her name out loud.

"I'm dying," he whispered brokenly, not thinking he could last another minute. "I'm going to lose control."

"Not before I get a chance to ride."

It began. She withdrew partially, then plunged back on him again, taking him deeply inside of her. Over and over, thrusting her hips, rocking her bottom, slapping flesh against flesh, drawing up her knees and arching her body to ride harder. Each time she took him back inside of her, he seemed to go deeper still.

Mark grasped her hips, trying to hold himself inside of her but it wasn't working. She was determined to ride him and all he could do was give in and meet her movement for movement, thrust for thrust, stroke for stroke.

His gaze locked on hers and what he saw in their dark depths sent even more heat rushing through his body.

He released her hips to curl his fingers in Alli's hair and gritted his teeth against the intense pleasure that was overtaking his body. He needed to kiss her, join her mouth with his but, before he could do so, she cried out his name. It was then that he let himself go and was thrown into a climax the depths of which he had never experienced before. His release kept coming and coming and she kept riding and riding.

She cried out his name again and threw her head back. Then after thrusting hard one final time, she collapsed on his chest. After a few moments, he felt her body go slack and could tell she was about to drift off to sleep. He wrapped his arms around her while trying to recover from what had to be the most exquisite experience of his life. He wanted to hold her in his arms for the rest of the night.

"How did I do?"

Mark groaned as a chuckle escaped his lips. "Sweetheart, if you would have done any better, I'd be a dead man."

All he could think about was the way she'd looked on top of him, riding him to her heart's content with the potency of her scent tantalizing his senses, her head thrown back, her firm and perfect breasts jutting forward, her hair tumbling wildly and swaying with every motion of her body as it moved up and down over his.

He took a deep breath as an overwhelming sense he'd never felt before caused his body to go taut and something inside of him came close to shattering. Closing his eyes and tightening his jaw, he forced the foreign feeling aside.

With a confused groan, he buried his face in Alli's throat as he fought to stop his control from slipping any further. He reminded himself that this was all he and Alli could ever share.

No matter what, he could not let her get past his defenses.

Ten

A week later, Alli stood on the sidelines and watched Mark instruct a class of women on the art of self-defense. Her throat felt tight and her pulse escalated as she watched how he moved with precision, causing his broad shoulders to flex under his T-shirt. His firmly muscled thighs encased in a pair of sweats demonstrated incredible energy whenever he hunched down or let out a kick with lightning speed.

She swallowed thickly, amazed at how much Mark continued to appeal to her on a primal level. Intense heat rushed to pool between her thighs and she shifted positions to find relief. The cool air blasting from a vent overhead wasn't much help.

As she continued to watch him, she couldn't help but think of how things were between them. A smile tugged at the corner of her mouth when she remembered the picnic they'd had a few days ago. Mrs. Sanders had urged them to get out of the house and enjoy themselves while Erika was taking a nap and had gone so far as to pack a lunch for them.

Mark had driven them to a section of Hartman land near a huge lake, and after spreading a blanket on the ground under an oak tree, they had sat down. She had enjoyed eating the sandwiches while listening to him share his days of being in the marines and the close relationship he and his brother had with her. He even had talked about his mother and what a loving and thoughtful woman she had been. Alli noted that he avoided any conversation about his father or his deceased wife. But what she remembered most of all was them making love beneath the low hanging branches of that oak tree.

Alli's thoughts shifted to how she and Mark had gotten into the habit of sharing a bed every night. But a tinge of disappointment touched her heart when she thought of the shield he continued to keep not only with her but also with Erika. It seemed as though this boundary was elementally necessary for him to maintain a detached persona. But she had seen him let his guard down a few times, but quickly he would resurrect it.

"Da-da."

She glanced down at Erika who was sitting in her stroller getting excited at seeing Mark. No matter how many times Mark corrected his niece, Erika was intent on calling him daddy.

Alli hunched down to Erika. "He's busy now, sweetheart, but he knows you're here and will come over as soon he's finished." Alli had taken Erika shopping that morning for some winter clothes and while in town she'd decided to drop by the studio.

A few minutes later when class was over, Mark glanced over in their direction and smiled. The expression on his face indicated he was glad to see them. He ducked under the rope that kept the observers off the gym floor and walked over to them.

"Hello, ladies."

Alli smiled. "Hi, yourself." She felt her pulse go haywire again. God, but he smelled good. Only with him did sweat mix with a magnetic male force to produce a scent that was physically overpowering. She wished that for once he would defy proper etiquette and pull her into his arms—something he would do if they were behind closed doors.

"Erika and I were wondering if we could tempt you to have lunch with us at the Royal Diner," Alli said, forcing her brain to function normally.

He glanced at his watch. "I wish I could but I have a few things I need to do around here. Maybe some other time."

She caught her bottom lip between her teeth and glanced down at Erika to hide her disappointment. "Sure."

She glanced up to see him looking at Erika. That's when Alli saw it, a deep longing to pick up his niece, plant a kiss on her cheek and cuddle her close. But Alli knew that he wouldn't. To do so would show emotions and he had been taught as a child that to expose himself that way was a taboo.

He met her gaze, and at that moment, although she knew that he didn't feel anything for her, she felt all the love she had for him. The degree shook her to the core.

Realizing that they were standing staring at each other, she broke eye contact and returned her attention to Erika. "Well, I guess we'll be going."

"All right. Thanks for dropping by."

Alli glanced around. "Things seem to be running pretty smooth here without me."

He hesitated only the barest second and then said, "Don't ever think you aren't needed, Alli."

His words sounded breathy and Alli had to force herself not to put much stock in them. However, she couldn't resist cocking her head to the side and asking, "You sure?"

He nodded and said, "I'm positive."

Her heart suddenly lodged tightly in her throat. "We better be going. It will be time for Erika's nap pretty soon."

"All right."

"Da-da."

Alli couldn't help but smile. It seemed that Erika didn't intend to be ignored.

Mark hunched down. "You're ready for lunch, little lady? Uncle Mark can't go this time, but maybe next time."

Alli shook her head. Now it had gone from just *Mark* to *Uncle Mark*. "We'll see you at dinner, Mark."

He straightened and met her gaze again. "All right. Enjoy lunch."

"We will." She pushed Erika past him and kept walking without looking back.

Later that evening while Alli was giving Erika her bath, Mark came home. He had called to let Alli know that he would miss dinner. Nita Windcroft had contacted him. She had received another threatening letter and the Texas Cattleman's Club had met to discuss it.

"I can't believe someone is still harassing Nita," Alli said as she leaned over to take Erika out of the tub. Squealing at the fun she'd been having, Erika kicked up her legs and splashed water on both Alli and Mark.

Laughing, Alli wrapped Erika in a thick towel and handed her to Mark. "I washed now you can dry." She ignored the surprised look on his face.

"So what did the note say this time?" she asked, walking out of the bathroom to go to Erika's bedroom with him following behind.

"More of the same. The message is always vague. This one said, *Get out or else.*"

Alli turned and raised an eyebrow. "If someone thinks a few notes and a little mischief will force Nita to leave her land, then they are crazy. I just hope you guys do something before Nita has a mind to take matters into her own hands."

Mark nodded as he continued to dry Erika. "I'm going to turn the note over to Gavin to see if the person who wrote this is the same one who wrote all the others."

He handed his niece back over to Alli. She'd noticed that lately Mark avoided any physical contact with Erika whenever he could, yet he had confided in her once that, when he had first gotten Erika, he would spend time rocking her in the rocking chair. It seemed to Alli that he had a tendency to put up a boundary when he found himself getting too close or when he felt his emotions were becoming involved.

"I left dinner warming for you in the oven."

"Thanks."

"Once I get Erika dressed for bed, I'm going to rock her for a while. You can join us if you'd like."

"Why?"

She shrugged. "I thought that perhaps you'd want to spend some time with her before she goes to sleep."

He looked at her for a moment, then at Erika and said, "No, that's not necessary." Without saying anything else he walked out of the room.

Alli walked through the French doors that led out onto the patio where the pool was located. She had put Erika to bed and had gone looking for Mark only to discover he had eaten and was in his office going over the ranch's accounting books. Deciding not to disturb him, she had gone to her bedroom to change into her bathing suit. She felt tense and thought a little swim might help.

She'd swum a dozen or so laps when she decided she'd done enough. Releasing a contented sigh, she climbed out of the pool and began drying herself with the huge velour towel when she glanced over and saw Mark standing in the doorway.

She met his gaze. "How long have you been standing there?"

"Long enough."

"Long enough for what?" she asked.

"Long enough for me to realize how much I want you."

Alli found herself melting under Mark's intense stare. There he stood, leaning in the doorway wearing a pair of stonewashed jeans and a T-shirt. She wondered if he knew he had a patent on the word *sexy*. Without batting an eye she asked, "So what do you plan to do about it?"

The wantonness of her invitation was so unlike her, but so were a number of her actions since she had moved into this house with him to become Erika's nanny. There was something about Mark that brought out something within her that she hadn't known existed. It was as though beneath the layers of flesh that covered her lived a passionate, insatiable being.

"Haven't you learned by now never to tempt me?" he asked, beginning to walk toward her.

As soon as he came closer into the light, she saw just how much he wanted her. She could barely draw breath into her lungs. The lower part of his body that she knew would soon be connected with hers looked bigger than she'd ever seen it before. All from watching her swim?

He stood directly in front of her and reached out to take the towel from her hand and toss it aside. "I want you so bad I actually ache, baby," he whispered in her ear.

She was beginning to ache, too. The sexy sound of his voice, his breath hot against her skin wasn't helping matters. "Then I think I better help you find relief."

She lifted up his T-shirt, then smoothed her fingertips against the bare portion of his waist before easing them lower to the fastener of his jeans. She began undoing the zipper, and when that was done, she worked her fingers inside the waistband of his jeans. Her pulse increased at the feel of his hot, turgid flesh.

She caressed him, remembering the first time she'd done so and how aroused he'd gotten because of it. She moved her fingers back and forth, thinking there was something deliciously naughty and decadent about having him in her hands this way. She might be putty in his hands, but right now, at this very moment, he was the opposite of putty in hers. He was as solid as a rock.

"Your touch is driving me crazy," he whispered and

seemed to grow larger in her hand. "I got to have you. Now!" he growled as if in pain.

Before she could draw her next breath, he had pushed her hand aside and snatched down the top of her bathing suit, freeing her breasts. But he didn't stop there. Determined to see her completely naked, he lowered his body to remove the suit entirely. Then he stepped back, ripped off his T-shirt, followed by the quick removal of his jeans and briefs. The sound of foil being torn rent the silence and she watched as he prepared himself, not for the first time wondering how such a small condom could fit over anything so big.

Heat of the highest intensity rushed to pool between her thighs when his hand suddenly reached out and went there, at the same time that he pulled her close to him and began sucking on her breasts. She shuddered, already so close to climax with the feel of his fingers stroking her between her legs and his mouth making a treat of her breasts. Her shivers became so intense that it was becoming hard for her to stand upright.

"Mark!"

"Not yet, baby, just hold on for a little while longer."

That was easy for him to say, she thought as his assault on her became more intense, more pleasurable. The feelings he was causing to flow through her were too great and she didn't know how long she would be able to hold on.

"Can't last until we get to the bedroom," he growled in her ear as he walked her backward until the backs of her legs touched the daybed and they tumbled on it together. She reached out to touch him but he shook his head. "No, not yet. There's something I have to do. It's something I've dreamed of doing to you for a long time."

Before she could ask what that something was, he dropped to his knees in front of her and curved her legs around his shoulders. He looked at her and she saw how his hazel eyes darkened and heard how deeply he was breathing just moments before he dipped his head between her legs, pressing an open-mouth kiss to her womanly core.

When the tip of his tongue touched her, she thought she was going to moan her throat raw, and when his tongue began twirling around inside of her, then licking and flicking out torture of the most sensuous kind, she threw her head against a huge fluffy pillow and instinctively raised her hips against his mouth. "Yes…oh yes."

What words she muttered after that she couldn't remember, but she was sure she said, *Please, don't stop, go deeper,* and *Yes, right there.* The intimate kiss grew more intense. It was as if he were hungry and planned to feast on her all night. She had heard about men and women engaging in this special form of lovemaking, but had never in her wildest dreams thought she would ever indulge in anything like this. Mark was proving her wrong. And when the swift signs of an orgasm began taking over her, she couldn't help but scream, grateful that Erika's bedroom was on the other side of the house.

"Mark!"

And then he was moving over her, parting the slick flesh that he had kissed greedily just seconds before. He entered her, sinking inside of her to the hilt and filling her completely.

"Hold on, baby. We're about to test this daybed's endurance," he said, pinning her arms above her head and smiling when her breasts jutted out. He began feasting on them at the same time the thrusts began. He pumped his throbbing arousal into her and pulled it back out again, over and over. And each time he filled her, he absorbed the shivers that hit her body with the impact. It seemed her womb was contracting with every stroke of his manhood.

Each time he withdrew, her hips followed him, almost coming off the bed, refusing to be disconnected from him, only to have him thrust back inside of her. When she heard him growl out her name, he let go of her arms and grasped her hips.

"Alli!"

She watched how he gritted his teeth, stretched his neck and threw his head back as an orgasm rammed through him. He pulled out slightly but was thrusting back inside of her again, gripping her hips, refusing to sever the connection and she knew he was having yet another climax.

Watching his intense pleasure spurred her into another one and her fingers dug into the muscles of his shoulders and almost instantly she cried out. Words she had held back for two years found their way out of her throat and she heard herself saying, "I love you, Mark," just moments before another shudder worked its way through her body and she was entrenched in the throes of total fulfillment.

She had literally driven him wild and the shock of it jolted right through Mark. But what was even more detrimental were the words she had whispered while having an orgasm...*I love you, Mark.*

The sheer shock of her words had sent him into a

panic. He didn't want her to love him. Want him, yes. Need him, yes. But love him, no.

Alli was the kind of woman a man could, and should, love but Mark wasn't the one to do it. He had issues to deal with and they were issues that the rest of his life wouldn't resolve. He looked down at her. So that both of them could fit in the daybed, her body was spooned intimately against his. She had drifted off to sleep. He studied her features and wondered how a sleeping woman could look as if she were ready for the next round of making love.

He sighed deeply. She was not supposed to fall in love with him. There was no place for love in his life, which meant there was no place for her in his life, either. He should have known, should have expected. Alli wasn't the type of woman who would give her body to a man without believing that her heart was involved. He had made a humongous mistake in letting his desire for her get in the way of his better judgment.

Long moments later, he listened to her even breathing and he knew what had to be done. Picking her up into his arms, he carried her into her bedroom and placed her in her own bed. After placing the covers over her, he stood back, deciding since she'd slept in the nude before, he wouldn't wake her to put on a nightgown.

Mark knew that the intimacy the two of them had shared during the past three weeks would always be a part of him. The thought that he was the first man ever to make love to her was truly special and at no time would he ever regret what they had shared. But there could never be anything lasting between them. He was a man who understood duty and not love.

After Patrice's death he had made a vow never again to let a woman matter to him and he meant to keep it.

The bedroom shone in the brightness of the morning sun by the time Alli awoke the next morning. She sat up and glanced around.

She was in her bed.

She lay back and drew in a ragged breath as she recalled in vivid detail what she and Mark had done just moments before she'd fallen asleep. She didn't need the fact that she'd slept in the nude to remind her. Ever since they had made love that first time, she had shared his bed so why had he brought her in here? She stared up at the ceiling trying to remember anything that could have happened to make him…

Then she remembered. She closed her eyes as she recalled the words she'd whispered to him while coming apart in his arms. She opened her eyes and pushed herself back up in a sitting position. Was this going to be his way of denying what she'd said? Did he think just because he wasn't one who was prone to show his emotions that she shouldn't show hers, either?

Alli winced at the thought that yes, that's exactly what he believed. He was no more interested in the fact that she loved him than he was in whatever was going on in Midland. And why should he when he had conveniently closed his heart ever to loving anyone again?

"Eat."

Alli forced her thoughts aside when she heard the sound of Erika on the monitor. Moving quickly, she got out of bed and headed for the bathroom. She and Mark would have a lot to talk about when she saw him.

* * *

She didn't see Mark at all that day and she was trying hard not to think that he was avoiding her, although deep down she knew that he was. Before, even when he would be away from the ranch for long periods during the day, he would call and tell her his schedule, and more than once he had surprised her and Erika by dropping by for lunch. But today he did neither.

The only highlight of her day had been a call she had gotten from Kara. Kara had told her all about her date at the movies. Alli had heard all the happiness and excitement in Kara's voice and it hadn't taken a rocket scientist to know that Kara was really taken with this guy.

Over the past couple of days, Alli had decided to let her sister live her own life and learn from her own mistakes. Alli was certainly learning from hers. It was true what everybody said about experience being the best teacher. And deep down she knew that Kara had a good head on her shoulders.

That night, Alli was in bed but not asleep when she heard Mark walk past her bedroom door going to his room after checking on Erika. At the sound of his bedroom door closing, she got out of bed and quickly slipped into her bathrobe. Leaving her room, she walked purposefully down the hall to knock softly on his door. When moments passed and he didn't answer, she knocked again, knowing he was there.

When he didn't answer after her second knock, she opened the door, stuck her head in and called his name. "Mark." She heard the sound of the shower running, figured he was in the shower and made the decision to wait.

He walked out the bathroom stripped down to his

jeans at the same moment she walked into his room and closed the door. She tried not to notice the fact that his jeans were unsnapped.

"What are you doing in here, Alli?" he snarled.

She winced. In all her years of knowing him, this was the first time he had used that tone of voice with her. "I need to talk with you about something. I knocked twice and when you didn't answer, I thought I'd just come in and wait for you to finish your shower."

He leaned in the doorway of the bathroom. "Does what you want to talk to me about concern Erika?"

"No."

"Then whatever it is will have to wait until morning. I had a rather tiring day today and—"

"Why are you doing this, Mark?"

He tilted his head and looked at her. "Why am I doing what?"

"Casting me aside."

He crossed the room in a second flat, grabbed her wrist and stood looming before her. Anger was etched in his features. "Do you think that's what I'm doing? Casting you aside? Don't you know that I'm trying to be considerate of your feelings, Alli? I heard what you whispered to me last night, and knowing how you feel, how can you expect me to continue when I can't reciprocate those feelings? I want you, but I don't love you. As for Erika, what I feel for her is a sense of duty which I intend to carry out as long as there is breath in my body. I owe it to Matt. I care for both you and Erika but love has nothing to do with it."

Alli took a deep breath. No matter what Mark was saying, he loved Erika. He did more than care. Since living in his home, Alli had observed him with his niece and, although he wasn't quick with the kisses and cuddles, he'd always been there, helping her with Erika's feedings, baths. Why couldn't he see what was so obvious? And why couldn't he believe that over time he could love her as well? She knew loving didn't come easy for him but she refused to believe he couldn't find it in his heart ever to care anything about her. There wasn't a time when they'd made love that he hadn't made her feel loved, whether he knew he was doing so or not.

"You can love someone if you let yourself do so, Mark," she said, believing her words as she said them.

He stiffened, then let go of her hand and stared at her for a long moment. "Is this what you've been about all this time? Did you take the job as Erika's nanny because you thought doing so would be a way to get next to me? And that eventually I'd think differently about how I feel about love?"

When she didn't say anything but continued to look at him, he said in a sharp tone, "Answer me, dammit. Did you?"

Unable to believe he would ask such a thing, pain ripped through Alli. She glanced at the bed, where they had shared numerous passionate nights, before meeting his gaze. She swallowed, fighting back the emotions that were thick in her throat. "The reason I'm here as Erika's nanny is because you said you needed me, Mark."

She quickly looked away. "I guess I heard you wrong." She met his gaze again and then said, "There is no reason for me being here other than that. Good night."

Without giving him a chance to say anything, she brushed past him and swiftly walked out of the room.

Eleven

"Are you all right, Mr. Hartman?"

Mark opened his eyes and released his hand from the bridge of his nose, glancing across his desk at his temporary secretary. He had been in the middle of reciting a list of things he needed for her to do next week when thoughts of Alli suddenly had consumed his mind.

It had been almost a week since their argument, which was the last time he had seen her. He deliberately was gone from the ranch by the time she got up in the mornings and he didn't return until way past her bedtime. He would check on Erika every night when he got in, and a couple of times he had paused outside of Alli's door. But knowing the way things were between them was for the best, he had quickly moved on.

"Mr. Hartman?"

The woman was staring at him strangely. "Yes, Mrs.

Roundtree, I'm fine. I just had a tension headache. Let's finish this later, all right?"

She nodded as she stood. "Yes, sir. Buzz me when you're ready to get started again."

Mark heaved a deep sigh and leaned back in his chair when Mrs. Roundtree closed the door behind herself. He knew that his accusations had hurt Alli and he wanted to kick himself in the rear end every time he thought of what he'd said. But at the time, he still had been in shock at the thought that she could be in love with him.

Although he believed that letting her know how he felt had been the right thing, he owed her an apology for some of the other things he'd said. He had been wrong to suggest she'd had an ulterior motive for taking the job as Erika's nanny. He knew the only reason she was there was that he had asked her to help him out. He had told her that he needed her and he still did.

When he saw Alli again, he would give her the apology that she deserved. She was the type of woman he should be running away from. She had been pretty clear that whenever she married she would want kids and he'd been adamant about not wanting any. She always would be the type of woman who would expect her husband to love her and Mark was incapable of loving anyone. With Erika, he was there to meet her physical needs, be her caretaker and nothing more. Why was it so hard for Alli to accept things?

His thoughts were jarred with the ringing of his telephone. He quickly picked it up. "Yes, Mrs. Roundtree?"

"Jake Thorne is on line one, sir."

"Thanks. Please put him through."

As soon as the connection was made, Mark said.

"Jake? What's up man?" He wondered if Jake's call had anything to do with them getting a possible lead on the Jonathan Devlin murder.

"I just left campaign headquarters and passed by the studio, saw your truck and wondered if you wanted to join me for lunch at the Royal Diner since Alli and Erika won't be at home."

Mark lifted an eyebrow. "They won't?"

"No, they're out shopping with Chrissie."

"Oh."

Jake chuckled. "Can't you keep up with your womenfolk?"

"No, I guess I can't."

"Trust me, it'll get easier."

Mark doubted it. He checked his watch. "I can join you in half an hour."

"That's good timing. I'll stop by the sheriff's office and talk to Gavin to see if there's news on anything."

"Okay, I'll see you there."

"Oh, look Erika, this is such a pretty playsuit and it's going to look so nice on you. I can even see you wearing it on Christmas Day," Alli said as she folded the newly purchased item to place in the drawer in the little girl's room.

Too bad I won't be here to see you in it, she thought as a pain settled around her heart. She had made her decision and it was final. During the past week, Mark had withdrawn so much, retreated into a shell, that not only was he trying to avoid her, but in doing so he was avoiding Erika as well. Alli couldn't let it continue.

As painful as it had been, she had gone to the Royal

newspaper office and placed an ad for someone to replace her as Erika's nanny. Once she felt comfortable the person Mark hired would work out, she would give him her resignation as both Erika's nanny and his administrative assistant.

She had decided that leaving Royal would be for the best. She had contacted a real-estate agent in Austin and, although she hadn't mentioned anything to Kara when she'd called yesterday, she was seriously considering moving there. With Alli's secretarial experience and good work record, it shouldn't be hard to find a job in Texas's capital. She had never lived anywhere other than Royal but felt that now it was time for a change. She hadn't told anyone about her plans other than Christine. Alli would tell Kara when she came home next weekend to get the car Alli had gotten for her.

The only thing Alli had to keep her going were the memories of the time she and Mark had spent together, alone and with Erika. Like the fuel she needed, she constantly replayed those special moments in her mind. And she believed that no matter what Mark thought, he was wrong. There was room in his heart for love but he was just too bullheaded to see it.

"Da-da."

Closing the drawer, Alli crossed the room and picked up Erika. "Your da-da hasn't forgotten you, little one. I know for a fact that he checks on you every night when he gets in. It's me he's trying to avoid, not you." She pulled Erika to her and hugged her tight. This little girl had come to mean a lot to her during the past three weeks and she would miss her dearly when she left.

But she had to do what she had to do.

* * *

Mark walked into the Royal Diner and glanced across the room. He saw Jake and quickly moved in that direction. Jake stood, stuck out his hand and Mark took it in a handshake.

"I was beginning to think you weren't coming, Mark," Jake said smiling. "I just finished talking with Chrissie and she says that Erika and Alli are back at your place. I might as well warn you that they spent a lot of your money."

"It was for a good cause I'm sure," Mark said pulling out a chair and sitting. Not wanting to discuss Alli and Erika any longer, he asked, "Did Gavin have any other news?"

A frown appeared in Jake's rugged face. "No, but he did mention that last note that Nita received was written by the same person who wrote the others."

Mark nodded. He was afraid of that.

"Excuse me, Mr. Hartman."

Both Mark and Jake looked up to see a young woman standing beside their table. She was not someone Mark recognized, and since she wasn't wearing a uniform, he knew she wasn't one of the waitresses. "Yes?" Mark said, rising from his chair.

"I was wondering about that ad in today's newspaper. Is the position still open?"

Mark's eyes widened in surprise. He knew nothing about an ad in the newspaper. "What position are you talking about?"

The woman looked at him strangely, then replied, "The one for a nanny. The ad said you were looking for someone and I've got a lot of exper—"

"There must be some mistake. I'm not looking for a nanny and I didn't place an ad in today's paper for one."

"Oh. The paper must have run an old ad by mistake then. Sorry to have bothered you."

Mark watched the woman walk off. Instead of taking his seat, he turned to Jake and said, "Excuse me for a minute. I need to snag Manny's newspaper to check out something." He returned a few minutes later with a deep frown on his face.

"Well?" Jake asked, leaning back in the chair. "Was it a mistake?"

Mark sighed deeply. "Evidently not. There is an ad in today's paper. I called the newspaper and they said Alli came in and placed the ad a couple of days ago."

Jake lifted an eyebrow. "She's quitting?"

"Apparently."

Jake tipped back his hat. "You really don't know what's going on with your womenfolk, do you? I found out the hard way that's the worst mistake a man can make."

Mark sighed deeply thinking that no, that wasn't the worst mistake a man could make. Being a total fool was. "I have to go, Jake," he said, already crossing the diner and heading for the door. The newspaper had to be wrong. Alli could not be leaving him.

"Where do you think you're going?"

Alli's hand flew to her chest. She had just walked out of Erika's room after placing her down for her nap, only to find Mark standing in the hall with an intense look on his face. "Mark, you scared me. I didn't know you were home."

"Answer my question, Alli," he said, struggling to control his temper.

Alli inhaled deeply. "Okay, we can talk in the kitchen."

He walked ahead of her and was pacing the kitchen by the time she got there. He stopped and glared at her. "All right, now where do you think you're going? We had a deal."

"Yes, and it's one I plan to honor so I'm not going anywhere, at least not until you find my replacement. Then I will be leaving. And just so you'll know, I'll be turning in my resignation as your administrative assistant as well. I've made a decision to leave Royal and move to Austin."

Her words were like a punch in the gut. He leaned against the kitchen counter to get his bearings. *She wasn't just leaving him, but was actually planning on leaving Royal?* "Why are you doing this, Alli?"

She took a deep breath as he continued to look at her. "To me it's simple. For two solid years I've loved you, Mark, and worked hard not to ever let you know it. It was my secret and my secret alone. I'd heard about what happened to your wife and knew there was a chance you might not ever get over her and it didn't matter to me if you didn't love me because I loved you and that's all that mattered."

She walked across the floor and sat at the kitchen table. "But that's no longer true. My feelings do matter to me. I came here to be Erika's nanny and it hurt that you thought I was manipulating the situation to be your lover. That wasn't the case, Mark."

He crossed the room to join her. "I know that, Alli,

and I want to apologize for insinuating such a thing to you. I was still shocked at what you'd said the night before, although that's no excuse."

She met his gaze. "No, it's not an excuse and as far as my emotions are concerned, my feelings are my feelings, Mark, and nothing you do or say will make me change them. However, I respect and appreciate your honesty about how you feel. Therefore, I think the best thing for me to do is to leave Royal."

When he started to say something, she held up her hand. "No, Mark. You need to understand something. I've spent a large portion of my life taking care of Kara. When you came to town I fell in love with you, and I honestly thought that loving you secretly would be enough. Until I moved in here and became your lover, it was. I was even willing to sentence my sister to the same type of life I had, all work and no play. That would have been wrong. There's beauty in loving someone, sharing your time and life with that person."

She paused briefly before continuing. "Now that I know how wonderful it is to love someone openly with no boundaries, I've decided that's what I want. My only problem is the man I love doesn't want me or love me back. So the only thing left is to pick up my pride and move on. I'm not a woman who can be a man's lover and not want something in return. I have to have love. I can't change the way I feel no more than you can change the way you feel. That's why it is best for me to leave Royal and start a new life someplace else."

She took a deep breath and slowly released it as she

stood. "Now if you don't mind, I want to get some rest while Erika is sleeping."

Not giving him a chance to say anything, she hurried out of the room.

Mark remained sitting in the chair long after Alli had left. Maybe leaving Royal would be the best thing for Alli since she deserved better. But why did the thought of her leaving cause a colossal pain to settle deep in his heart? The thought of never seeing her again was something he just couldn't bear. He thought about how his relationship with Patrice had been and knew what he'd shared with Alli had been so different. Was he going to go around blaming himself for the rest of his life for Patrice's death, knowing things might not have been any different had he been in the States? He and Patrice had begun living separate lives even while residing under the same roof. He had offered to teach her self-defense many times but she had refused his offer.

He thought of all the things he and Alli had shared. There was such a goodness about her that went beyond how she took care of Erika. It went beyond how she'd taken care of her sister and, more importantly, it went beyond how she had taken care of him.

And she had taken care of him. Since she had moved to the ranch, he had experienced some of the happiest and most joyous moments of his life. Suddenly he was struck with the reason why.

He loved her.

There was no sense denying it. As much as he hadn't wanted to fall in love with her, he had, and he could be honest enough with himself to admit he had probably loved her for as long as she had loved him. But since coming to live in his home, she had shown him love and how to express it, with her and with Erika. And he wanted to continue what they shared. It no longer bothered him that Erika referred to him as her father. When she got older, he and Alli would tell her all about her parents and how much they had loved her and that Matt had entrusted her in Mark's care because deep down his brother had known that eventually he would show her love and not expose her to the loveless childhood they had endured.

He stood, knowing what he had to do. He had to convince Alli that he loved her and wanted her as part of his life.

Alli had sworn she wouldn't cry but was doing so anyway, she thought as she wiped tears from her eyes. Moving away from Royal wouldn't be so bad. Austin was a big city with a lot of opportunities. She would make new friends and, who knew, she might even meet someone whom she could learn to love.

Fat chance! Her heart would always belong to Mark.

She lifted her head off the pillow when she heard a knock at her bedroom door. Knowing it could only be Mark, she ignored it. There was nothing left to be said. When she heard the knock again, she decided to see what he wanted. Definitely not her, she thought.

With a heartrending sigh, she crossed the room to open the door. "Yes?"

"I listened to what you said in the kitchen and now I'm asking that you listen to what I have to say."

Alli glanced down at the floor, not wanting him to

see her red-rimmed eyes. Besides, she couldn't look into his face without seeing the man she loved more than anything. Feeling somewhat composed, she finally looked up. "I'm sure your message will be the same, Mark, so why bother?"

"Please hear me out, Alli."

Instead of saying anything, she backed up to let him in. He walked over to the window and looked out a long moment before turning around to face her. "The one special memory I have of my mom that I'll always hold dear to my heart was the day she took me and Matt for a walk. I believe it was the same day the doctor had given her the news that she only had a short time to live."

He looked out the window for a moment again and then his gaze returned to Alli. "She told us the story we'd heard so many times before about how our grandparents found oil making them rich. She also said that it was her dream that that legacy would continue with our kids. It wasn't until years later after she'd died and I was raised by a father who didn't know the meaning of expressing love that I decided I would never marry nor would I have children."

He walked across the room to lean against her dresser. "While serving in the marines, I met Patrice through a friend. Her childhood had been just as rough and unloving as mine, and because of a medical condition that had left her sterile, she couldn't have children. What we entered into was more of a partnership than a real marriage. Neither of us knew how to express our emotions and we were fine with it."

He looked down at the floor a moment then back at Alli. "I'd been satisfied until Erika came into my life. I kept wanting to give her more of myself but didn't think that I could. The one thing I didn't want was for her childhood here with me to resemble the type Matt and I had with our father. But it was only until you came to live here that I could see how much distance I'd put between me and my niece, even when I hadn't meant to do so."

He crossed the room to stand before Alli. "I'd never been my happiest, Alli, until you came to live here with us. I thought I could go the rest of my life without love but I see I can't. Knowing you might be leaving Royal has knocked some sense into me. I love you, Alli. I love both you and Erika, and I don't think I could handle it if you were to leave. Stay here, marry me and make this place a home for us. I want the three of us to become a family. I told you once that I needed you. At the time I didn't know how much. Now I do. If you will have me, I will never give you a reason to want to ever leave again."

Alli's mouth trembled and she swallowed a lump caught deep in her throat. She was speechless after Mark's declaration of love.

"I'll be good to you and our daughter. I promise."

Alli blinked back her tears. "Our daughter?"

"Yes, I want us to adopt Erika and when she gets older we will tell her all about Matt and Candice. I think they would have wanted things that way."

"What about other children? I want them but you don't, Mark."

"I do now," he said softly, meaning every word. "I want to give you my babies, Alli. As many as you want. I want to be a father to our kids, a good and loving father who won't be afraid to show them how much I love them every day of my life."

Alli squeezed her eyes shut to stop the flow of her tears and dipped her head. Mark's words were making her dream come true. He reached out and tilted her chin up with the tip of his finger. "I love you, Alli. Will you marry me and continue to show me love in its purest form?"

She met his gaze, saw the hopeful look in his eyes. "Yes," she said tearfully. "I love you, too, and I want to marry you so you, Erika and I can be a family."

He pulled her into his arms and held her close to his heart. "I love you, Alli," he said for the third time that day. "Everything will work out between us and we will be a family."

She smiled up at him. "Yes, we will be a family."

He pulled her into his arms, tasting the tears on her lips. And this time he put all the emotions he'd ever held back into this kiss, wanting her to feel the love that was flowing through every vein in his body. Desire ran rampant through his blood and he needed to make love to her, claim her as his, connect with her, and let her know just how much she was loved.

He picked her up in his arms, sweeping her off her feet, and carried her over to the bed. Without uttering a word, they undressed each other and, when they were both naked, he placed her against the pillows. He thought she was the most beautiful woman in the world lying nude before him with her hair spilled over the aqua bedspread.

She reached out for him. "Make love to me, Mark."

He came to her, drew her tongue deep into his mouth, sucking on it until she groaned out. His hand went lower down her body, past her stomach to settle between her legs and found her wet, ready, hot. Pulling back, he quickly sheathed himself with a condom and then moved his body in position over hers.

He met her gaze. Held it. And when he began entering her, he knew he had come home. When he'd gone as deep as he could, he kept his body motionless, needing to feel her around him, clutching him, loving him. Then with a loud animalistic growl, he withdrew, then thrust back into her again, feeling her body shiver and shudder at his onslaught. Over and over, he withdrew and went back in, knowing this would be his home for the rest of his days. And that she was his woman.

He spread her thighs some more, grasped her hips to part her farther, then threw his head back as flesh slapped against flesh, the sound heating up their desires and passion even more.

"Mark!"

She screamed his name, once, twice, three times and he continued to move within her. Then he gritted this teeth as a howl burst from his lips and he frantically rocked his body into hers, needing to go as deep as he could with the woman that he loved.

And he did.

Mark rolled off Alli to stare at the ceiling as he fought for breath. They had made love several times before, but never with this intensity. He pulled her into his arms. "I love you."

She looked over at him and smiled, fighting for breath as he was. "I love you, too."

"I want to get married next weekend, Alli."

She let out a soft chuckle. "Rushing things, aren't you?"

He grinned. "Yes, I suppose I am. Do you think it can be arranged?"

She sighed upon seeing he was dead serious. "I'll call Kara. She was coming home next weekend anyway to get her car so that time might be perfect."

"Good, and when Erika wakes up we'll go to the jeweler so you can pick out a ring. We're going to make it a family affair."

Alli smiled. "That sounds wonderful to me."

"Da-da. " Erika's voice could be heard through the monitor.

Alli smiled sheepishly. "Oops. My screams may have wakened her."

Mark chuckled. "Or it could have been the sound of this bed knocking against the wall."

"Mark!"

"Well, it's the truth," he said laughing.

"Da-da."

Mark leaned over and flipped on the speaker that was connected to Erika's room. "Your daddy is coming, sweetheart," he said with all the love in his heart.

He glanced over at a smiling Alli. An expression of love and tenderness consumed his features when he said, "And so is your mommy."

Four days later, a smiling Mark walked into the Texas Cattleman's Club to attend a meeting that had been called by Gavin. It was a perfect Texas night and back home waiting for him were two perfect young ladies. Everything was set. He and Alli would be getting married this coming weekend. Her sister would be there as well as all of their friends. Mrs. Tucker had called two days ago to let them know she would be returning to Royal and would love to have her old job back as Erika's nanny.

Mark and Alli had jumped for joy and, since Mrs. Roundtree was working out just fine at the studio, he suggested that Alli attend school full-time to obtain her degree. When she finished, he wanted her to use the vacant space in the studio as her computer-engineering business office.

"Hartman, wipe that silly grin off your face so we can get down to business," Logan said when Mark took a seat at the table.

"Hey, don't get testy because I decided not to have a long engagement and move ahead and marry my woman. I expect all of you to be at the wedding on Saturday."

"We'll be there," Gavin said grinning. "Now let's get down to business. With this last threatening note to Nita Windcroft if things continue to escalate, one of us may need to start watching the Windcroft farm. I think Connor would be the logical choice. With his army ranger experience he will be the perfect person for the job."

Jake leaned back in his chair. "Have you broken this news to Connor yet?" he asked, thinking that his brother would have his hands full taking on Nita Windcroft. He wouldn't wish that nightmare on his worst enemy.

"No, and I don't plan to do so, either, until he returns from Virginia. This is something he needs to hear in person."

Everyone nodded in full agreement.

"Connor did indicate he wanted me to call him tonight and place him on speaker phone so he can personally congratulate you, Mark, since he won't be attending the wedding. He's still tying up loose ends."

Mark nodded, understanding.

"And we all decided," Jake said, standing, "Since all of us are here and Connor will be shortly by way of speaker phone, we'd end this meeting and turn it into a bachelor party. Everything has been set up downstairs."

Mark laughed. "Thanks, guys."

Gavin leaned back in his chair. "Any advice for die-hard bachelors?"

Mark grinned. "If you find the woman you want, don't let anything stand in your way of getting her."

Both Jake and Logan, who also were engaged, nodded in full agreement.

Gavin rubbed his chin and said, "Hmm, that's interesting advice."

Tom smiled. "It sounds pretty damn debatable if you ask me."

But all the men later agreed that a woman was something none of them could live without.

Epilogue

All eyes were on the couple on the dance floor sharing their first dance as man and wife. The wedding reception at the Hartman Ranch had been in full swing for almost an hour and everyone present had to agree it had been a beautiful wedding for such a gorgeous couple. The bride was wearing a long white bridal gown and the groom was wearing a black tux. Alli's sister, Kara, had been her maid of honor and Christine had been her bridesmaid. Jake had been Mark's best man.

Mark and Alli would be leaving later that night for a flight that would take them to Dallas and from there to Hawaii, where they would spend the next week. They couldn't imagine being away from Erika any longer than that. They were thankful that Mrs. Tucker had arrived and would be taking care of their precious darling.

Mark tightened his arms around Alli. He felt as if he

were the luckiest man alive and looked forward to being a good husband to Alli and a wonderful father to Erika. He intended to spend the rest of his life showing both of his ladies just how much he loved them.

"Nita looks nice doesn't she?" Alli asked.

Following her gaze, Mark saw Nita Windcroft talking to Mrs. Tucker. She was wearing a light blue pantsuit. "Yes, she does and this is the first time I've seen her in anything other than a pair of jeans."

Alli nodded. This was the first time she had seen Nita wearing anything but jeans, too. Alli thought the pantsuit looked really good on Nita and couldn't wait for the day she got to see Nita wearing a dress—if that day ever came. "So, Mr. Hartman, are you ready to take time away from Royal for a while?"

"As long as I am with you, Mrs. Hartman, I am ready for anything." He leaned closer and kissed her, ignoring the catcalls and applause.

When he released her, Alli glanced across the yard at her sister, who was smiling happily at her. Alli smiled back. Cameron, who had arrived in town with Kara to help her drive her new car back to Houston, was indeed a hottie. But after talking with him, Alli concluded that he was also a really nice guy. He had come from a family of attorneys and had plans to go to law school. She could tell he cared a lot for Kara and he told her that he and Kara had talked about it and had decided not to let their dates interfere with their schoolwork. Alli liked that decision. Even Mark had said he liked Cameron since he seemed to be a pretty decent and mature guy with a good head on his shoulders.

Moments later, when Mark escorted her back to their

table where Erika was sitting in her high chair, he leaned over and kissed his niece. Love ran swiftly through Alli's veins as she watched her husband. He was no longer afraid to show his emotions and for that she was thankful.

Hand in hand, they began walking around thanking their guests for coming and sharing in their special day. Happiness shone on their faces in knowing this was the beginning of their lives together and they intended to make every day exceptional.

"How about another dance, sweetheart?" Mark asked, pulling her into his arms and leading her toward the dance floor.

"I'd loved to," she said, smiling up at him.

He leaned down and brushed a kiss across her mouth. "And I love you," he said softly, thinking he could never say it enough. Never had he dreamed someone so beautiful would come into his life and help him to overcome his past, and give him the love and the passion he'd always yearned for. He gathered her closer into his arms and couldn't wait for later that night when they would be alone.

"What are you thinking about, Mark?" Alli asked, leaning back slightly to look into his eyes.

His eyes—no doubt full of love—held hers. Deciding that what he was thinking about was for her ears only, he leaned closer and whispered to her.

What he said nearly took her breath away. He smiled and hugged her closer, burying his face in the curve of her neck and inhaling the scent that was so much a part of her. "You did ask."

A smile touched the corners of Alli's lips. He had just

whispered some very naughty things that he had planned for her later. "Yes, I did, didn't I?"

"Yes, you did," he murmured softly. And then he was kissing her again.

* * * * *

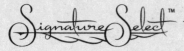

COMING NEXT MONTH

#1681 THE HIGHEST BIDDER—Roxanne St. Claire
Dynasties: The Ashtons
A sexy millionaire bids on a most unlikely bachelorette and gets the surprise of his life.

#1682 DANGER BECOMES YOU—Annette Broadrick
The Crenshaws of Texas
Two strangers find themselves snowbound and looking for ways to stay warm, while staying out of danger.

#1683 ROUND-THE-CLOCK TEMPTATION—
Michele Celmer
Texas Cattleman's Club: The Secret Diary
This tough Texan bodyguard is offering his protection…day and night!

#1684 A SCANDALOUS MELODY—Linda Conrad
The Gypsy Inheritance
She'll do anything to keep her family's business…even become her enemy's mistress.

#1685 SECRET NIGHTS AT NINE OAKS—Amy J. Fetzer
When a wealthy recluse hides from the world, only one woman can save him from his self-imposed exile.

#1686 WHEN THE LIGHTS GO DOWN—Heidi Betts
Plain Jane gets a makeover and a lover who wants to turn their temporary tryst into a permanent arrangement.

SDCNM0905